IS HERE THERE?

여기가 거긴가?

Journey of a Diaspora Artist

IS HERE THERE?

JAE WON LEE

디아스포라 작가, 길을 묻다

여기가 거긴가?

IS HERE

이재원

CONTENTS

목차

PRELUDE

들어서는 말

a book project

This is about a small book making "process" around 2019–2023. Rather than being an artist's catalogue full of refined photographs of finished work, it offers a glimpse into a time of confinement, a big move during COVID-19, relocation, and constant departures without a destination. It covers the artist's bi-cultural journey, artmaking, creative processes, material selections, selected results, trains of thought, and wanderlusts. Producing a book involves planning, organizing, and publishing within the given time. But it also takes an endless period of confronting the "self," a process one usually wants to avoid.

I find tall stacks of written memos, studio notes, diaries, and sketches on all kinds of papers and notebooks. There is neither order, nor consistency in chronology or places, but I attempt to put it together into a small book. It might prove quite difficult as my verbal and writing skills are awkward in both English and Korean. Korean typing is almost impossible. And what about awkward translations? So, it looks like this book making process will be slow. A headache. . . . Should I quit now?

Double/Multiple personalities: Korean mind versus American mind versus the mind in between. Through my bilingual writings, I realize the split personality and distinctive personas divided by two languages and cultures.

Where does the first word begin? A word has dictionary definition, but it may contain slightly different meanings depending on personal interpretation. Put a word in place, arrange it with another, make a sentence with selected words. When a person meets another through the medium of writing and they focus their attention on the same thing, they become companions. Which word will be the one to help us connect? Moreover, the title—the book's name—should be chosen.

책 만들기

책자를 하나 만들려고 한다. 완성된 작품의, 정교한 사진 위주의 카탈로그 말고, 2019년에서 2023년 사이,
지난한 코로나 기간 중의 감금과 이사, 이주, 귀국[역이민], 또 새 보금자리를 찾아 종착역 없이 출발만
지속되는 방랑의 시기에 대해. 이는 또 한 미술인의 이중 문화의 여정, 작업, 과정, 재료 선택, 작품,
일련의 사고[思考]와 배회한 거리에서 든 생각, 방랑벽에 대해 끄적거린 메모, 작업 노트, 일기를 중심으로
솔직하게 엮은 신변잡기 기록이다. 주변 공간, 어지러운 작업장, 새로 시도한 작업 사진을 곁들여...
주어진 일정 기간에 계획, 정리, 인쇄가 가능할까, 밑도 끝도 없는 자아, 문젯거리들과 마주해야 하니,
피하고 싶은 과정이기도 하다.

끄적거려 놓은 메모, 작업 노트, 일기 등등이 한 묶음이다. 두서도, 연계도, 시간과 공간을 관통하는
공통점도 없지만, 이들을 버무리고 엮어서 작은 책으로 만들 엄두를 내본다. 한국어와 영어, 두 언어로
쓰자니, 두 언어에 모두 어눌한 사람인데, 한타는 그야말로 '올모스트 임파서블'. 또 번역의 어색함은
어쩌랴? 그러니 이 과정은 무지 느릴 듯. 고민이다. 지금이라도 관둘까?

이중-다중인격: 한국적 마음 vs. 미국적 마음 vs. 낀 마음. 이중언어로 글을 쓰면서, 나는 두 언어와
문화에 의해 분열된 성격을 마주치면서, 나와는 차이 나는 다른 인격의 내재를 깨닫는다.

첫 단어는 어디에서 시작하나? 단어에는 사전적 뜻이 있으나 개인의 해석이 담긴 약간 엇나간 의미를
부여할 수는 있다. 단어에 위치를 주고 배열하여 더 고른 단어들로 문장을 지어 공유한다. 글로 사람과
사람이 만나고, 한곳에 시선을 두면 동행인이 된다.
우리를 이어줄 첫 단어는 무엇으로 할까. 책 이름도
지어야겠지.

9

self-portrait [multi lens] | 지화상 2019

Introduction

While attending a liberal arts college, studying psychology in Seoul, I came to the United States and have since settled here for quite some time as an artist. At first, there was a language barrier, then there was a piercing anguish that could not be explained in words. I did not pursue the language of visual art to express myself, but serendipitously entered the path of an artist. After studying sculpture at California State University, Long Beach and ceramics at New York State College of Ceramics at Alfred University, I have been expanding the scope of my work by going back and forth between the US, China, Europe, and Korea. Although initially starting with ceramics, I have been straddling the boundaries of various visual genres by taking on multiple roles: 2D artist, mixed-media artist, object maker, potter, ceramic sculptor, installation artist, curator, and art teacher. I have been on the tenure-stream faculty at Michigan State University [MSU] since 1998.

Above all, the plants and everyday objects naturally existing around us form the subject matter of my work. I reflect on life as an immigrant, my origin, and identity. Through lyrical and delicate artwork, I express my thoughts and longing for Korea, my motherland. In particular, the shape of a lunch box or a book wrapped in an embroidered handkerchief in my *Immigrant Flowers* series, carries the narrative of a wrapping cloth that embraces and wraps everything. It symbolically depicts the emotion of *jeong* [a Korean term for the warm feeling of love, sympathy and attachment that forms between people who share an emotional or psychological bond]. The *Moon Shadow* series, consists of layered fragments of lace, hair knots [using strands of hair, I tied countless knots], remnants, and trash elements, was created by stitching together or layering sheets of translucent and transparent paper to create an image resembling an Asian landscape. *Flower buds that bloom in a foreign land—Blooming Somewhere Else,* is a porcelain panel series featuring cut-outs from printed tissue paper that are carefully transferred

소개

서울에서 대학의 문과 계열, 심리학과 다니다가, 도미, 오랜 기간 미국에 정착하여 현재까지 활동하고 있는 나는 미술작가다. 처음엔 언어장벽, 후엔 가슴에 사무치는 내뱉을 수 없는 말. 그래서 딱히, 시각적 언어로 표현할 방도를 구한 건 아니나 우연찮게 미술인의 길로 들어섰다. 캘리포니아 주립대 조소과를 거쳐 뉴욕 주립 알프레드 대학원 도예과를 졸업하고, 미국과 중국, 유럽, 한국을 오가며 작업의 영역을 넓혀 나가고 있다. 도자에서 출발했지만, 미술인으로서 나는 평면 작가, 도예가, 조각가, 설치작가, 큐레이터curator, 미술 선생의 역할을 수행하고 있고, 1998년부터 미시간 주립대학의 교수로 재직 중이다.

무엇보다도 우리 주변에 자연스럽게 존재하는 식물, 일상의 사물을 작품의 소재로 끌어내어, 이민자로서의 삶, 나 자신의 근원에 대한 사유, 그리움과 같은 소재들을 서정적이고 섬세한 작업으로 표현하려고 한다. 특히 꽃수를 놓은 보자기로 도시락을 싼 형태를 도자로 제작한 "이화[離花, 이민자들의 꽃]"는 모든 것을 포용하고 감싸는 보자기의 의미를 활용해 '정[情]'이라는 정서를 상징적으로 보여주려고 했다. 레이스, 쓰레기 조각과 머리카락, 자투리 등을 층층이 겹쳐 올려 바느질하거나, 반투명, 투명 종이 사이사이에 겹쳐 동양의 산수화와 같은 이미지를 연출한 "달 그림자-Moon Shadow" 시리즈와 전사지를 세심하게 오려 도판 위에 전사한 작품 "타지에서 맺을 꽃봉우리-Blooming Somewhere Else"는 장식적인 느낌보다 절제된 색채와 세밀한 구성으로 미니멀minimal 하고 고요한 느낌을 담으려고 했다.

흙 표면에도 바늘 자국을 내고 종이나 섬유 작업에도 바느질을 하니, 작업장에선 바늘이 손에 노상 잡혀 있다. 바느질, 눈이 침침하다시면서도, 할머닌 옷 수선하시랴, 수놓으시랴 밤늦도록 바느질을 하셨다. 꽃수에 나비나 새는 꼭 둘씩이다. 난 어린 나이에도 얼굴도 모르는, 오래전에 돌아가신 할아버지를 할머닌 그리워하시나 보다 하고 생각했다. 할머니는 자기만의 시간에 행복한 꿈나라를 수놓으시나 보다라고. 난 내 식의 바느질에 몰입하면 화해의 마음을 얻게 된다. 작업실에서 한참 작업하다 보면 자각하게 되는 체험이다. 작업 중 치유의 경험을 한다. 나의 작업을 접하는 이에게 한순간만이라도, 마음에 고요한 동요가 있음 좋겠다. 소란스러운 마음이 평온해지기를 바란다.

11

onto ceramic tiles. Rather than having a decorative appearance, this minimal piece and its restrained colors carry a feeling of serenity.

I hold needles in my hand all the time in the studio—marking the surface of clay or stitching on paper and textile work. Sewing. Even though it was hard on her eyes, grandmother would sew late into the night while mending her clothes or embroidering. Butterflies and birds appeared in pairs among her embroidered flowers. Even at a young age, I assumed grandmother missed her long-dead husband whom I had never met. It seemed as if she was embroidering her happy dreamland in her own time. When I immerse myself in my personal style of sewing, I sense a feeling of reconciliation. It is an experience that takes some time to gain after working in the studio. It is an experience of healing. My wish is that all those who encounter my work experience a moment of calm stirring within, no matter how briefly. May one's noisy heart find peace.

Between Pages, pressed flowers in a book | 책갈피 속에 말린 꽃잎

Granny's lucky pouch　|　할머니 복주머니, circa 1974

나는 시를 둘러싼 빈 공간을 응시하고,
흰 곳 아래 어딘가에서 숨겨진 단어가 나오기를 기다린다.

I stare at the blank space around a poem, waiting for the hidden words
to emerge from somewhere under the white.

Moon Shadow | 달 그림자 [책 한 권]

It all started with the expression "Hither and Thither [here and there]."

The title of the book *Is Here There?* was conceived upon my return to Korea in May 2023, when the fragrant scent of acacia flowers in the wind transported me back to my childhood. As I hummed the song, "Homeland" from my childhood, following the white acacia petals fluttering in the wind with my eyes, the lyrics "There where the blue sky ends, is my homeland there?" gave me the idea for the title. Back in my days in Long Beach, the West end of America, I would gaze at the horizon from the beach, asking myself, "Is that—way over there—where Korean land begins?" So, now that I'm here, back on Korean soil, is this the land I so longed for? Is here there?

As I'm trying to write, I don't know what to do with all the old memories rushing back to me. When I was little, my mother and grandmother spoke the Gyeongsang-do dialect, and Seoni who helped out with housework spoke the Chungcheong-do dialect. I had a good ear for dialects and was quite good at imitating the quaint accents before being sent off to America as a young adult where I became mute and deaf in the English-speaking country. Here, I got by on *nunchi* [the subtle art of gauging others' moods and needs] alone.

It would break my parents' hearts to hear me say that, throughout my childhood, I grew up feeling out of place, constantly second-guessing myself, but that was what being a second daughter was like. My older sister, like all eldest daughters in Korea, was deemed a household asset, a lucky charm. Meanwhile, my one-year-younger brother, like all sons in this blatantly son-preferring country, was just an excuse to sing hooray and throw feasts and my youngest sister was, well, the youngest. My parents had already achieved a son, so she was just an added bonus, while all I was, was a fifth wheel.

사족

"이리저리"가 첫 단어가 될 것 같다.

책 제목으로, "여기가 거긴가"는, 올해 5월 한국에 다시 오니 아카시아 꽃내음이 바람에 날리던데,
향긋한 꽃내음 덕에 동심으로 돌아가, 그때 부르던 동요 '고향땅'을 흥얼대니, 바람에 날리는 아카시아 흰
꽃이파리에 한눈팔며, "푸른 하늘 끝 닿은 저기가 거긴가"에서 착안. 미국 땅 서쪽 끝 롱비치 해변에서
멀리 수평선 바라보며, '저~어기가 거기, 한국 땅인가, 자문하던 시절로 돌아가. 여기, 한국 땅에 왔으나,
그리움의 나라, 거기가 과연 여기인가, 여기가 거긴가?

Here and There [Hither & Thither], exhibition title | 이리저리

As I've come to accept, my life began not with a warm welcome, but with despondent interjections of disappointment. "Again? Another daughter?" Even growing up, some people would mock the angry and woeful child that I was for being more attached to my grandmother, saying "Your mom is your grandmother. You're your grandmother's child." When describing inhospitable treatment, Koreans use the expression "being served cold rice," but the treatment I got was comparable to being served spoiled rice. As if the second-daughter's destiny of being constantly sidelined wasn't enough, I also had to be born in the Republic of Korea, a nation that relied on agriculture as its national stabilizing force. Moreover, I was born at dawn in April in the Year of the Ox [April marks the beginning of sewing season for farmers and the Ox symbolizes diligence and hard work.] and was therefore fated to labor my life away—which I did. For someone like me, who resists digital technology in favor of the analog, an artist who insists on handwork, I am constantly drained by physical, mental, emotional, and academic labor.

When I first started college in the United States, my eyes were teary every night as I would sulk in self-pity, resenting my father. My high Test of English as a Foreign Language [TOEFL] score eased me into an American school, but as someone accustomed to Korean-style rote learning, America's creative-thinking, individuality, and open discussion-oriented education terrified me. The credits I earned from my Korean university, with the exception of physical education credits, were nullified with the transfer—now, that's what we call "clearance"—and I was degraded from a junior to a freshman. I even had to drop my liberal arts course in the middle of my first semester to take English as a Second Language [ESL], a course that contributed no credit towards graduation—for two semesters. My friends in Korea at this time were preparing for graduate school or going on blind dates with prospects of marriage. Being pulled back five years to become a not exactly old, but rotten freshman left Lee Yongbok's "Mother, Why Did You Have Me?"—a song I would mindlessly sing as a child—ringing in my ear. Becoming unable to speak and listen, the painfully tragic lyrics cried by the blind singer who always

글을 쓰려니 밀려오는, 옛 기억들을 어쩌랴? 유년 시절엔 할머니와 엄마의 경상도 사투리, 집안일 도와주던 선이 언니의 충청도 사투리가 귀에 쏙쏙 들어와, 들리는 대로, 구수한 사투리를 제법 잘했는데... 다 커서, 영어 쓰는 미국으로 보내져, 벙어리, 귀머거리같이 지냈으니, 눈치껏 살았다고 해야 할까?

워낙 어려서도 눈칫밥 먹고 자랐다면 우리 부모님 억장이 무너질 터이나, 내 입장에선 둘째 딸이란 순번이, 위치가 그러했다. 위로 언니야 맏딸이니 살림꾼 복덩이, 연년생 남동생이야 남아 선호 사상 노골적인 우리나라에서, "남동생 만세." 동네방네 잔치 났지. 막내 여동생이야 막둥이, 이미 아들 하나 있으니 '웰컴 투 코리아.' 난, 낙동강 오리알.

나의 태어남은, 필시, "또? 또, 딸이야?", 환대는커녕 실망 어린 허탈한 물음표로 시작된 삶이려니. 자라면서도 할머니와 더 가까이 지내니, 화나고 구슬픈 내게 "니네 엄만 할모니야, 넌 할모니 딸이야!"란 조롱. 찬밥보다 못한, 쉰밥 신세 아니었을까? 암튼 눈칫밥 꽤나 먹을 둘째 딸 운명이다가, '농자천하지대본 [農者天下之大本]'이라고, 농사가 천하의 근본이며 나라를 안정적으로 유지하는 힘이라고 여기는 우리나라 대한민국에, 소띠, 춘사월, 새벽 생이라니, 일복은 엄청 타고난 모양이라, 노동을 업으로. 나처럼 디지털은 안 하는 아날로그인, 손 작업만 고집하는 미술인은, 육체적 중노동에, 정신적, 심리적, 학문적 고심에, 심신이 항상 매우 고단하다.

처음, 미국 대학에 다니려니, 매일 밤 눈물이 앞을 가렸다. 갖은 청승 떨며 '아부지'만 원망했더랬다. 토플 시험은 잘 봐서 어렵지 않게 편입은 했으나 언어 장벽 외에도, 암기 위주의 주입식 교육에만 익숙한 나는 창의적, 개인적 사고 위주, 열린 토론의 미국 교육에 질겁을 했다. 한국 대학 학점은 체육만 빼고 편입 학점 이수 '제로zero' 처리라니, 이른바 '땡처리'가 따로 없다. 3학년이었던 난 '프레시맨freshman'으로 강등. 첫 학기 중간에 필수 교양 과목 포기, 졸업 학점에 전혀 도움이 안 되는 '제2언어로서의 영어, ESL' 반에서 두 학기. 한국에 있는 내 친구들은 대학원 준비다, 선을 본다 하는데... 5수생이나 진배없는 '쉰'[rotten, 썩은] '프레시 맨'이라니, 소시적, 아무 생각없이 따라 부르던 가수 이용복 님의, "어머니, 어머니, 왜 나를 낳으셨나요?" 나 자신이 귀머거리, 벙어리 신세라서, 짙은색 썬글라스 끼고 절규하듯이 노래하던 한 사람의 애절한 사연이 남의 고통만이 아니었다.

대학 졸업장 하나 따는 데 10년 걸리니, 남들은 박사 학위 딸 시간인데. 매해 전공을 바꿔대는 딸년에, 아버지는 울화통이 치밀어 속이 타들어 가고도 남으셨을 터. 난 나대로, 한국에서 대학 졸업하고, 내가

19

wore pitch-black sunglasses felt as if they were my very own. It took me 10 years to earn a college diploma—enough time for most to earn an additional master's degree. My father must have flared up several times in frustration, left with ashes for a heart as he watched his lamentable daughter switch majors year after year, which isn't to say that it was any less frustrating from my end. I resented my father for not letting me finish college in Korea, for not understanding that bachelor's degrees in America are much harder earned than master's degrees, for not giving me the option of pursuing a master's degree abroad at my own will if I felt the need, for never asking me before abruptly sending all four of us siblings away then moving to another country themselves. Oh, there were bursts of anger. With the four of us split up and moved to our schools of choice and the family torn apart, I came to realize that we all groaned our way through life, each struggling with the weight of our own grievances. But since I now understand, if only belatedly, the circumstances that cornered my father into his decisions, I guess I've finally grown up. Finally, after passing the age of 60.

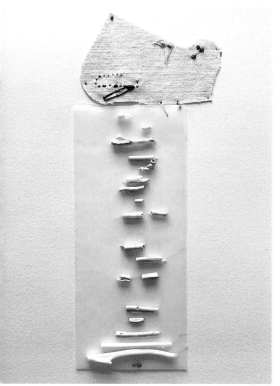

tag ends, 2023 | 자투리 2023

원하면 대학원 유학이나 보내 줄 일이지. 미국
대학 학부 졸업은 대학원 과정보다 훨 어려운데.
나한테는 물어보지도 않고, 갑자기 독단적으로
우리 사 남매를 미국으로 보내고 부모님은 또 다른
나라로 가시냐, 울화통. 우리 넷은 각자 학교를
정하게 되어 뿔뿔이. 이렇게 찢어진 가족이라
각자의 어려움에 각자의 고충의 무게로 인해 우리
모두는 속으로 신음하면서 살았구나라는 생각도
이제야 든다. 하지만 그럴 수밖에 없던 아버지의
사정을 때늦게 헤아리게 되니, 이제야 철이 드나
보다, 환갑도 넘은 나이에. 쯧쯧.

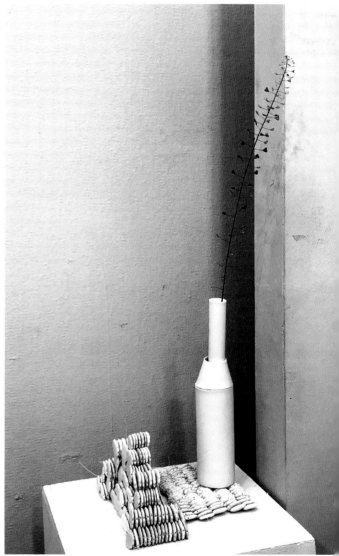

corner | 구석

LOCKDOWN

자가 격리

February 2020–May 2023, Big Moves

House. I am determined to move to a different state and become a full-time artist by the time I complete my 25-year tenure at Michigan State University. I had planned since 2019 to execute various moving projects one by one, starting in 2020, the year of my sabbatical leave. The biggest challenge was the sale of the house. I lined up handypeople for house repair, painting, and pruning large trees, but suddenly the COVID-19 disaster spread to the entire world.

With the exception of essential visits to hospitals, pharmacies, and grocery stores during the lockdown enforced in the US, the doors of all other businesses shut down. All outdoor activities were prohibited. Followed by sudden announcements of staying home and teaching online? Thus, all the moving-related jobs were dumped on me to suffer through. . . . A kind I can't express with words. . . . Moreover, the house was untidy from belongings I'd accumulated over the years as I went about my busy, everyday affairs and multi-tasking. The sale of my house led me to give up ownership and reduce the scale of life, furniture, belongings, and artworks. To this farmhouse built in 1867, a humble two-story brick house with its own distinctively countryside feel, I added modern touches for my own comfort and reflected my personal tastes in each and every room. As it was such an old house, there were always problems inside and outside, so I dedicated myself to the repairs and restoration as if it were a large artwork. While cleaning and organizing the house in preparation for its viewing, I felt as if I was presenting it as I would a solo exhibition.

2020년 2월~2022년 5월, 대이사

집. 미시간주립대학교 근속 25년 채우면, 교수직을 박차고 타 주로 옮겨 전업작가 하리라 벼르다가
안식년인 2020년에는 구체적으로 실행에 옮기려고, 2019년부터 차근차근 계획. 가장 큰 과제는 집 파는
일로, 수리와 페인트칠, 큰 나무 전지 도와줄 인부들도 알아봐 두었는데, 갑자기 코로나란 재해가 온
세상에 만연하는 불상사가 일어날 줄?

COVID 19 자가격리 때문에 병원, 약국, 식료품 가게 필수 방문을 제외하고, 모든 비즈니스 폐쇄. 외출이
전면 금지되어 갑작스런 재택 근무에, 온라인 수업이라뇨? 아니, 아니, 안 돼요! 그로 인해 집수리를 나
혼자 '뒤집어쓰게' 되어 생고생, 아니 개고생... 필설로는 표현이 안 되는... 게다가, 물건들은 점점 불어나,
바쁜 일상사에 쫓겨 늘어놓고 살다가 집 판다고 살림 규모를 줄이느라 눈물을 머금고 내놓은 가구들,
물건들, 작업물들. 1867년에 지어진 농가farmhouse, 2층 벽돌집 고유의 소탈함과 시골스러운 순박함에
나의 현대적 감각을 더해, 내 편의와 취향에 맞추어 작품 만들듯 정성 들여 손보지 않은 곳이 없는
집이었다. 고옥이라 늘 문제가 잇따르니 집 안팎과 마당 곳곳에 온갖 정성을 기울이며 큰 작품 대하듯
살아왔다. 부동산에 내놓으려고 단정하게 정리정돈하니 집으로 개인전을 하는 느낌이었다.

fixing bathroom, wallpaper, painting corner of room

Conflict & Dilemma

The word for conflict in Chinese [葛藤], is a combination of two characters meaning arrowroot and wisteria. Arrowroots grow counterclockwise and wisterias grow clockwise. Therefore, when they grow in the same place, the plant that climbs late strangles the plant that climbs first. But it does not die at the roots. Our society and world coexist despite numerous conflicts of interests, hostility, or conflicts between complex individuals or groups. Conflict is also within me. I must confront a circumstance in which a choice must be made between two equally undesirable alternatives: here or there, sell the house now or wait, resign now or delay? Should I or should I not?

I'm planning a move, but none of the specifics are set. In this enormous land that is the United States, I must leave the Midwest for the West, and then head to the East, harboring even more changes as I attempt to emigrate back to Korea. The COVID-19 disaster caused major disruptions to the processes of the long-planned move, in turn causing a great deal of conflict for the unknown scenarios of the entire world.

In the end, I sold my Mason house after living there for 20 years, surely the longest I'd stayed in any one place. The process of retirement from home ownership was more arduous and painful than I could have ever imagined. Repairing and beautifying the house, downsizing, organizing belongings, and working with a realtor to put a house on the real estate market was followed by the grueling task of packing my life into countless cardboard boxes. As soon as my house was sold, the aftermath of the real estate market fluctuated so intensely that prices doubled in northern Washington state, where I wanted to relocate. I found myself in a big dilemma regarding my relocation. I didn't know what to do now that getting out of Michigan was delayed from 2020 to 2021–22. I was stuck. . . . Left to just reflect on early retirement and my eventual relocation.

갈등. 진퇴양난

갈등[葛藤]이라는 단어는 한자 칡 갈[葛]과 등나무 등[藤]이라는 글자의 조합으로, 칡과 등나무가 서로
반대 방향으로 한 나무를 감고 올라감에 기인하는 것이야 잘 알려진 사실. 칡은 시계 반대 방향으로
나무를 감으며 올라가고, 등나무는 시계 방향으로 올라가는 덩굴식물이다. 그러나 칡과 등나무가
한곳에서 같은 나무를 타고 자라다 보면, 늦게 감고 올라간 식물이 먼저 올라가는 식물의 줄기를
누르게 되고, 그래서 먼저 올라간 줄기는 눌려서 서서히 죽는다는 건 누구나 다 아는 상식은 아니다. 또
그렇다고 해서 뿌리까지 죽는 건 아니고 죽은 줄기 위에 새순이 올라와 다시 나무를 감고 올라간다. 세계
어느 곳이든 인간 사회에서는 각각 다른 이해관계로 복잡하게 얽힌 개인이나 집단이 서로 적대시하거나
충돌을 일으키며 엄청난 갈등 속에서 공존한다. 갈등은 내 안에도 있다. 어떤 선택의 기로에 시종일관
의견을 달리하는 내면의 칡과 등나무의 얽힘으로 심사가 뒤틀린다. 둘 다 바람직하지 않은 대안 사이에서
선택을 해야 하는 상황에 직면한다: 여기 또는 거기?, 지금 집을 파나 기다리나?, 지금 은퇴하나 연기하나?
이사 계획을 세워보지만, 구체성이 결여돼 있다. 큰 땅덩이 미국에서 중부를 떠나 서부로 가야지 하다가
동부로 바뀌더니, 타 주로의 이사가 아닌 '이주'라는 거창한 포부로 바뀌어 한국으로 역이민을 갈까 하는
생각이 든다. 2020년 코로나 재앙은 오랫동안 이사move, moving를 계획한 내게 엄청난 차질과 내적
갈등을 유발하며 적잖은 내상을 입혔다.

우여곡절 끝에 나는 무려 20년 동안, 내 인생에서 가장 오랜 시간을 머물렀던 메이슨Mason 집을
팔았다. 집 소유주 은퇴 과정은 내 알량한 세상살이 역량으로 감당하기에는 힘들고 고통스러웠다. 집을
수리하고 단정하게 꾸미고, 물건을 정리하고, 부동산에 집을 내놓고, 중개사의 도움을 받아 마침내
매수자가 정해졌다. 다음은 셀 수 없이 많은 골판지 상자에 내 인생을 포장하는 지난한 일이 기다리고
있었다. 집이 팔리자마자 부동산 시장이 요동을 쳐 워싱턴주 북부의 점찍어 놓은 집값을 두 배로 올려
놓았으니, 나는 진퇴양난에 빠졌다. 2020년이 아니라 2021~2022년에 미시간을 떠날 계획이어서 새로
들어갈 집을 미리 장만하려 했건만, 나는 갇혀버리고 말았다. 그냥 이른 은퇴와 이사에 대해 아무 현실성
없는 공상이나 하며 찌그러져 있었다.

So long, farewell my house | 잘 있어, 나의 집

bye my bell flowers | 안녕, 방울꽃들아

NBF [new best friend], Dongyi

"Do not look back. A flying bird does not look back." Why look back while flying forward?

When I finally left my empty house of 20 years, the discomfort hit me—more than the joy of selling a house did—and quickly turned into a deep sorrow. I have been suffering from the physical, emotional, and psychological aftereffects for some time.

In summer 2020, I moved temporarily to a third-story apartment overlooking a big lake where a group of two to three hundred geese visited every morning. They would swim, play, and rest all day then suddenly fly away in the evening only to fly back the next morning, landing lightly on the lake. I experienced seeing hundreds of geese at once when I had never imagined seeing so many geese together in my lifetime, and the sight surprised me every morning. Their long necks stretched forward, and large wings flapped up and down as they created a splendid V-shaped pattern, high in the sky. After learning about how they take turns as the "leader" in the V-formation and that mating pairs of geese are monogamous for their entire lifespan, I was even more fascinated by these waterfowl. They became a source of consolation for me during the isolation of the COVID-19 lockdown. I'm quite grateful to those geese for keeping me company from a distance.

From the hundreds of geese, one in particular drew my attention—a goose with dam-aged wings whom I named Dongyi [東伊: Eastern One]. As Dongyi couldn't fly up to the sky, Dongyi remained all alone, walking around before disappearing into the darkness. Wondering where Dongyi slept all night, I tried to chase Dongyi, only to fail each time. Surely a child must be afraid of being alone. Would Dongyi be able to survive the harsh winter in Michigan?

As I watched a bird that couldn't fly while working on a piece titled *Blind Bird*, I empa-thized with Dongyi.

동이[東伊, NBF, 가장 친한 새new or bird 친구]

뒤돌아보지 마라. 날아가는 새는 뒤돌아보지 않는데. 왜 날면서 뒤를 돌아보겠어?

20년 간 살아온 집을 텅 비우고 떠날 때, 섭섭함이 시원함을 누르더니 이내 슬픔으로 변하여 가슴이 미어졌다. 신체적, 감성적, 정신적 타격을 엄청 받아 후유증을 오래 앓고 있다.

2020년 메이슨Mason의 집을 팔고 임시로 랜싱Lansing의 3층 아파트로 이사하니 창밖으로 호수가 내려다보인다. 아침마다 한 200~300여 마리 기러기 무리가 날아와 온종일 자맥질하다, 놀다, 또 놀다가 저녁때가 되면 모두 어디론가 날아간다. 내 전 생애를 통틀어도 볼 수 없을 수백 마리 기러기들을 한꺼번에 보는 호사를 매일 누렸다. 그 긴 목을 앞으로 쭉 뻗고 큰 날개를 휘저어 V자 형태를 만들며 하늘 높이 날아가는 무리. 그들이 V 패턴pattern을 이루는 무리의 리더 역할을 돌아가며 한다는 사실과 평생 일부일처제를 유지한다는 사실을 알게 되면서 나는 이 새들에게 더욱 매료되었다. 훌쩍 떠났다가 슬그머니 돌아오는 이 기러기 무리가 코로나 자가격리 상황에서 혼자 뚝 떨어져 고립무원의 처지에 있던 나에게 큰 위로가 되어 주었다. 장한 녀석들 참 고맙다.

녀석들 중에 양 날개가 상해 있어 유독 시선과 관심을 더 많이 끈 아이는 '동이'다. 나처럼 해뜨는 쪽에서 나타난 녀석이라 동이[東伊]라고 이름 지었다. 날지 못하니 뒤뚱거리며 걸어 다닌다. 해 질 무렵 다들 날아가면 동이만 혼자 남아 뒤뚱거리며 돌아다니다가 어둠 속으로 사라진다. 도무지 어디서 혼자 몸을 숨기고 밤을 나는지 궁금하여 찾아나서도 봤지만, 매번 실패. 혼자 두려움에 떨고 있지나 않을는지...

겨울이 오면 미시간의 혹독한 추위를 혼자 견뎌낼 수 있을까? 마침 "눈먼 새"로 제목을 붙인 콜라주collage 작업을 하던 차라 날지 못하는 새 동이에게 동병상련의 심정이었다.

Dongyi, the goose friend Solitude is exacting. | 동이

일부 미술 작품은 평평한 흰색 표면에 시 쓰는 듯한 나의 시각적 표현이다.

Some works are my way of writing a poem on a flat white surface.

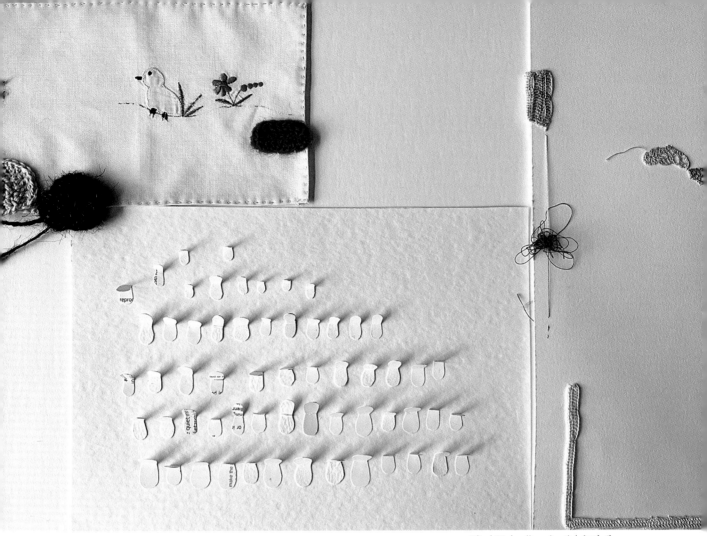

Blind Bird, collage detail | 눈먼 새

a good day: pond | 좋은 날

"Go back to your country!"

I was an undergraduate student in Los Angeles when the LA Riots broke out in 1992. Problems related to racism and ethnic insecurities have been daily experiences from day one of my life in America. When personal attacks were directed at me with severe hatred during the COVID-19 lockdown, my patience was exhausted and I thought, "Enough is enough. It's time to leave this country of racism." Finally, I attempted to leave the US and spend an extended period in Korea by applying to the Fulbright Research Scholarship. As the term "homing instinct" indicates, my current artistic research lies in the instinctual feeling that directs one "homeward" in both the philosophical sense—like from dust to dust—and the poetic sense of returning to a physical homeland or nature. Moreover, due to the pandemic lockdown, my psychological and emotional orientation became centered around my country of origin and on pursuing research and direct exchange opportunities in Korea. In this way, I returned to the country I'd been absent from for four decades, the place I felt increasingly alienated from during several brief visits.

funeral plates, Lausanne, Switzerland

"니 나라루 꺼져!"

L.A 폭동이 난 1992년에, 난 로스앤젤레스에서 대학에 다니고 있었다. 미국 생활 첫날부터 겪은 인종차별과 그로 인한 불안감은 일상이 되었다. COVID 폐쇄 기간에 심각한 인종증오와 폭력적 언어 공격이 직접 나에게 쏟아졌을 때, 인내심은 바닥이 났고 나는 "이제 충분해, 이 인종차별의 나라를 떠나자"라고 결심하게 되었다. 나는 미국을 떠나 한국에 장기간 있으면서, 아예 귀국하는 길을 모색하고 싶어 풀브라이트Fulbright 장학 재단에 응모하여, 교환 학자로 한 학기 동안 한국에서 연구와 교류의 기회를 부여받았다. '귀소본능[歸巢本能]'처럼 나의 예술적 작업은 '흙에서 흙으로 돌아가는', 어쩌면 아주 당연한 철학적 사고와, 고향과 자연으로의 시[詩]적인 귀향이라는 관점에 초점이 맞춰져 있다. 게다가 전염병 자가격리로 인해 심리적, 감정적인 지향성이 더욱 고국으로 향하게 돼 원래의 내 나라로 돌아왔다. 정주하지 않아서 40년 동안 부재했던 곳으로, 몇 번의 짧은 방문에서는 낯선 외지인처럼 느꼈던 곳으로.

good night, S & G | 잘자, 2000

funeral plates

WANDERLUST

역마살

Fulbright Blues

A return to your home country? After selling the house, I rented an apartment, then returned to Korea alone. I have no one place to call home. My condition is like that of a migratory bird. It reminds me of Dongyi. I also miss Sarojini and GgoMa [S & G], the cats whom I can't ever see again. S & G were little kittens that moved into the empty Mason house with me in 2000, and we lived there together for 19 years. Mysteriously, a month apart, these children breathed their last breath in front of my eyes and left this world peacefully. Brokenheartedly, I buried them next to a lilac tree in the sunny backyard, then I thought it's time for me to leave the Midwest, for a place I want to live in, where I won't feel like an exile. For me, it will be a long journey with great meaning. Even if I die on the road before I find such a place, what does it matter? It was such a heart-felt thing.

This is a different world. . . . Now I realize that although my body left 40 years ago, my heart remained intact here. After obsessing over and longing for Korea, I returned to the place I had dreamed of, but the true reason behind the return would likely be properly leaving this place. This time, with my heart too. It is not easy to feel empathy from the Koreans of today who have joined the ranks of developed countries. This country and I have changed so much that I feel like I don't belong here. If I leave Korea forever, will I be able to take my longing away? I am not confident. I am a stranger in Korea as well as in America.

During my time in Korea under the Fulbright research scholarship, I have been reflecting more on microaggressions, the verbal or non-verbal insults that occur without any intent to hurt others' feelings. It refers to the minute, unintentional discrimination that is almost invisible, like fine dust. One of the characteristics of micro-discrimination is that the person who discriminates does not even know that their words and actions are discriminatory. I think that even if we try to be sensitive, some of our verbal or non-verbal

풀브라이트 블루스

고국으로의 귀국? 집을 판 후 아파트에 세 들어 살다가 혈혈단신 한국에 돌아왔다. 나는 이제 집 없이 떠돌고 있다. 내 신세가 철새 같다. '동이' 생각이 나고 이제는 다시 볼 수 없는 사로지니Sarojini와 꼬마 GgoMa [S & G] 도 몹시 그립다. 사로지니와 꼬마는 메이슨Mason의 빈집에 2000년에 함께 입주한 아기 고양이들로, 19년을 동고동락하던 사이였다. 이 아이들은 신기하게도 한 달 터울로, 마지막 숨을 내 눈 앞에서 내쉬고 평온하게 떠났다. 무너지는 가슴으로, 아이들을 볕 잘 드는 뒷마당의 라일락 나무 옆에 나란히 묻어주었다. 이제 나도 중부를 떠나, 유배지같이 느껴지지 않을, 내가 살고 싶은 곳으로 떠나리라. 내게는 엄청난 뜻을 품고 떠나는 장도가 되리라. 어쩌면 영원히 그런 곳을 찾지 못하여 객사한다고 해도 그 또한 어떠리.

여기는 딴 세상... 이제 와 깨닫느니, 40년 전 나는 마음은 고스란히 여기에 둔 채 몸만 떠났다. 한국에 대한 그리움에 사로잡혀 있다가, 꿈에도 그리던 한국에 돌아왔건만, 이제 돌아온 이유는 아마 마음마저 이곳을 진짜로 떠나기 위함이리라. 선진국 대열에 들어선 오늘날의 한국 사람들에게서 정감은 쉬이 느낄 수 없다. 이 나라도, 나도 너무나 많이 변해버려, 나는 이곳에 속하지 않는 사람처럼 느껴졌다. 한국을 영원히 떠나면 그리움을 거둘 수 있겠나? 그럴 수 있을까? 자신이 없다. 나는 미국에서와 마찬가지로 고국 한국에서도 이방인이다.

41

frozen pond, Dongyi vanished, Lansing, Michigan

communication can be insensitive. Cultural humility means respecting others and accepting the fact that we do not know about others. It means adopting an attitude of trying to understand the culture of others. People with this attitude can recognize their own assumptions or prejudices about others from different cultural backgrounds. For this reason, the Fulbright experience led me to contribute to the international understanding of microaggressions on a personal level, from a place of respect and humility.

October 27, 2022. Damn, life in Korea is not easy. Will I be able to return to Korea and live as I'd hoped, or will I go back to the US and find a new place to settle down? I keep asking the same question every day and am unable to answer. I was trying to live a good life when I turned 60 and, after coming here, start my life as a full-time artist in earnest. Whether it's writing, handling clay, or sewing. . . . While in Korea, I cannot get rid of the feeling that I have become more dull, lazy, and wasted my time idly. So, my heart gets heavier and heavier. On the long journey home from a long journey back to my temporary home, I despaired of myself. There is no space for me here. I disappeared for the first time when I left Korea for LA and I'm disappearing once again even after returning to Korea. Hide properly, lest your hair give you away. [This references the song sung by the "seeker" in the Korean equivalent of hide-and-seek.]

나는 풀브라이트Fulbright 한국 체류 시 맺어진 상호 관계에서 '마이크로 어그레션micro aggression [미세한 공격 또는 차별]'에 대해 생각해 본다. 명백하게 차별을 의도하는 건 아니지만, 말 그대로 미세한 먼지처럼 보이지 않는, 의도하지 않은 차별이고, 모욕이다. 미세차별의 문제 중 하나는 차별하는 사람이 자신의 말과 행동이 차별이라는 것을 알지 못한다는 점이다. 한국에 있으면서 물질만능, 외모 지상 주의에서 비롯된 미세차별을 종종 겪기도, 목격도 하였다. 이 문제를 개선하기 위해 상당히 신경을 쓰고 노력한다고 해도, 우리의 언어와 비언어적 의사소통의 일부는 우리도 모르게 무신경하게 이뤄질 수 있다. 문화적 겸손은 우리가 다른 사람에 대해 모르는 사실을 받아들이고 존중하는 것을 의미한다. 다른 사람의 문화를 이해하는 태도를 가진 사람들은 다른 문화권의 사람들에 대한 자신의 즉흥적인 생각이나 편견을 인식할 수 있다. 여기에도 역차별이 존재하고 문화적 차이도 엄청나니, 무안할 때가 허다하다. 다름과 틀림의 차이를 곱씹는다.

2022년 10월 27일 젠장, 녹록지 않은 한국 생활. 내가 과연 원하던 대로 이 한국 땅에 돌아와서 살 수 있을지, 아니면 다시 미국으로 돌아가서 새로운 곳을 찾아 정착을 하게 될지 물음표만 연일 찍고, 딱히 답을 할 수가 없는 지경이다. 나이 60이 되면 제대로 살아 보려고 했는데, 여기에 오면서 본격적으로 작가의 삶을 다시 시작하자고. 글을 쓰든가, 흙을 만지고, 바느질을 하든가... 한국에 와 있으면서 오히려 더 무뎌지고 게을러지고 나태해져서 허송세월하는 느낌을 버릴 수가 없다. 그래서 마음이 점점 더 무거워진다. 장거리 여행을 하고 임시 거처로 돌아오는 긴 귀갓길에 나는 스스로에게 절망하였다. 여기에는 나를 위한 공간이 존재하지 않는다. 나는 한국을 떠나 L.A.에 갔을 때 처음으로 사라졌다. 나는 이제 다시 한 번 사라진다. 나는 한국에 돌아와서도 또 숨는다. 꼭꼭 숨어라, 머리카락 보일라.

Is Here There?

Period. Exclamation Mark! Question Mark? Comma,

If I were to say, "Here is There," the sentence would end, probably not with the degree of conviction implied by an exclamation mark, but at least with the sense of closure embodied by a period. But since I still feel unsure, the title has to be Is Here There? with a question mark at the end. Here is There! Here is There. Is Here There? Life in and of itself is a series of question marks, thus I always find myself lost and wandering.

I'm thinking about turning around and tracing my way back to where I came from. I grew up witnessing Korea's political transition from one military regime to another. It was the year before last that the villainous former president Chun passed [Here, I tried to write "croaked" or "went to hell," but I couldn't remember the correct Korean spelling, so I opted for a more modest expression.] Living with hate or holding a grudge does nothing but eat away at oneself, but this good-for-nothing person is more brute than man, and I abhor him with all my being. If it weren't for him, I might not have had to leave Korea in the first place. I spent my adult life with so much resentment toward my father, an authoritarian who looked up to the "self-elected president Park Chung-hee." He would make all the decisions for the subordinate members of the family to obediently follow [though he would never admit it], and I set out for America, suffocated by his sense of authority [though he would call it "love"]. I persevered, ran breathlessly to keep one foot off the American ground, dreaming of the day I would get to "go back." But as much as I thought about returning, it was easier said than done. Now that I've finally set foot on the path to reverse immigration, this doesn't feel right. I don't feel at home here either. Despite having anticipated this possibility, the reality is deploringly disappointing. So, here I am, left again in a state of quandary, unable to settle and in a constant state of uneasiness and confusion.

Hence, a comma. I might as well pause and take a break while I'm down. Speaking of commas, I'm realizing how frequently I use them in my Korean text as I do in English text.

여기가 거긴가?

마침표. 느낌표! 물음표? 쉼표,

'여기가 거기다' 라고 하면, 확신에 찬 느낌표는 아니더라도 마침표로 결론이 나겠으나, 여전히 '여기가
거긴가?'로 물음표를 붙여야 한다. Here is There! Here is There. Is Here There? 인생 자체가 물음표
투성이라, 맨날 헤맨다.

뒤집으려는 중. 왔던 길로 더듬어 가려고. 한 군사 정권에서 또 다른 군사 정권으로 바뀌는 한국 정치를
목격하며 어린 시절을 보냈다. 2021년에 그 전 아무개가 돌아갔다.[돼졌다, 뒈졌다? 철자를 정확하게
모르니 좀 고상한 단어를 썼다.] 누구를 미워하는 감정을 마음에 담는 것은 독을 품고 사는 것처럼
자해가 되는 일이나, 이 인간은 짐승만도 못하다, 너무 밉다. 이놈 아니었으면 한국 땅을 떠나지 않아도
되었을지 모른다. 나는 아버지에게 불만을 한가득 품고 살아왔다. 장기 집권 박통을 존경하시던
가부장적인 아버지의 '독재'. 모든 결정권은 당신께서 정해 놓고 아랫사람들은 명령에 복종하여 따르기만
하는[당신께선 부인할 듯하나], 아버지의 권위[그것이 당신께는 사랑이라는 명목으로 바뀔 터이나]에 눌려
숨통을 조이며 미국으로 향했다. 이제껏 숨가쁘게 땅에 발도 제대로 못 붙인 채 '돌아갈 날'을 꿈꾸며,
견디어 왔다. 돌아갈 요량이었지만, 그것도 어디 쉬운 일인가. 암튼 역이민의 길로 접어들었으나, 이것도
딱히 아니다. 한국 땅에서도 발붙일 여건이 아니로구나. 그러리라 추측은 하였으나, 그 정도가 훨씬
황망하니, 오호통재라! 그래서 진퇴양난이다.
우왕좌왕, 조변석개, 심난한 마음속은
쑥대밭이라...

Comma, 쉼표, 넘어진 김에 쉬어 가리.
그러고 보니, 내 한국어 글에는, 쉼표가 수시로
들어가네, 영어처럼. 당신의 직장, 장래에
대한 고민만도 엄청났을 터인데, 넷이나 되는
꼬물이들의 생계와 훗날 대학 공부까지 시켜야
할 책임감까지, 아버지가 짊어져야 했을 무게는
얼마나 되었을지 이제야 알아드린다. 이때는
아버지 나이 고작 40즈음 아니었겠나?

family photo | 가족사진

daddy | 아버지

HANDS-ON

수작

소중히 쓴 편지를 고이 접어 보내주니, 귀히 간직한다.
한국의 모시에 천연염색을 하여 한 땀 한 땀 정성을 들인다.
시간과 정성이 많이 들어간 작품에는 힘이 깃든다고 믿는다.

I cherish the precious, neatly folded, handwritten letters sent to me. I devote all sincerity to each of the stitches made on the natural-died Korean ramie. I believe that power indwells time and labor-intensive works.

I Got Your Letters │ 당신의 편지들은 잘 받았습니다.

again, hands-on

"The surface reality of clay or thread becomes subsumed in the macro view of the recurrent parts, while a telescopic examination of the individual components reveals a deeper image of the world.

"The white and clear line segments of thread float in nebulous fields that begin to gather into a narrative or healing force, then dissipate into the nonspecific. Seen mostly from the underside of the stitched surface, the scar of blister in the paper from thread pushing through often generates enough power to chew the paper into fuzz, particles released as frozen breath or clouds into the atmospheric space. What can we know of our human landscape until we look beneath the crackle of ice? Jae Won Lee has given us a view into the interior. The dead of winter is not dead; the complicit breath waits below the surface."

—from *Under Ice* by Gerry Craig

rheum, ellipsis, paper, thread

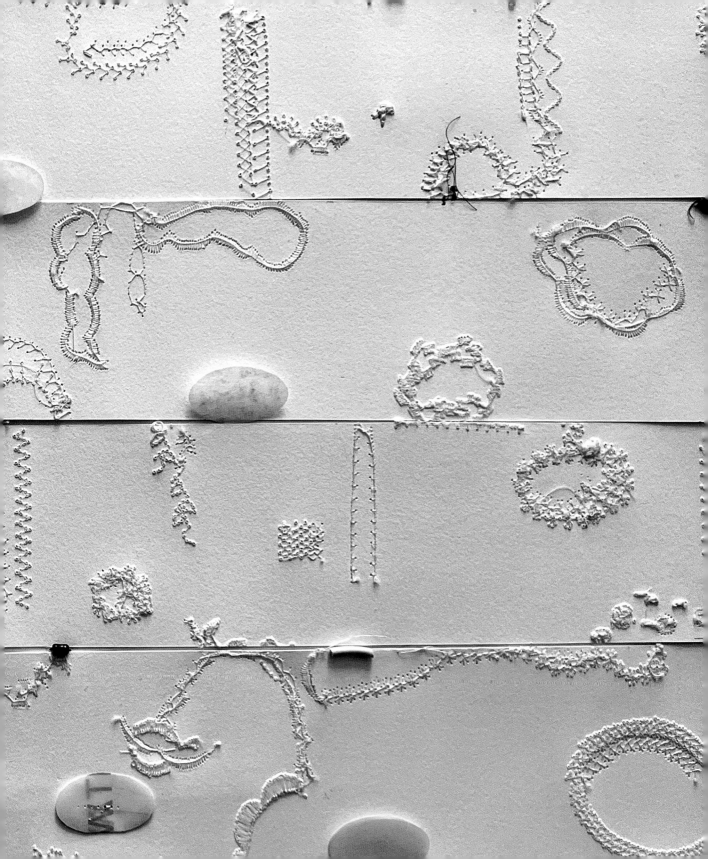

studio notes, winter

seeds,
silence.
solitude.
simplicity.

once everything was in the earth,
there was a lengthy period of waiting.
winter has become the right place to think.
there is so little out there.
it's a bid to be non-specific.
a view both elegantly pristine
and eerily absent of life.
the light-filled vision
of the snowy, frozen, or frosted landscape
seems to compress the atmosphere.
a stillness highly charged.
redefine the sublime.
to make visible the interior landscape,
journeying into self.

Collage on recyclable reproduction images of Miju Lee's paintings

다시 수작

[手作에서 秀作이거나, 아니면 酬酌]

수작-수작-개수작 전략 가능, 엉뚱하고 쓸데없는 짓일 수밖에...

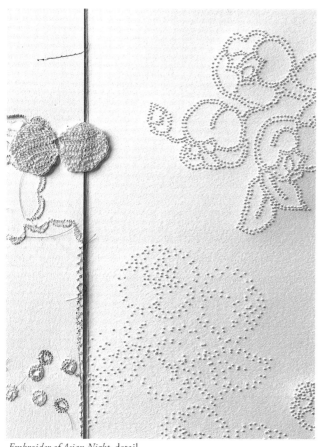
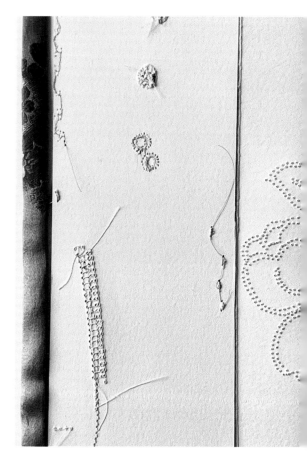

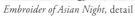
Embroider of Asian Night, detail

rheum [the smaller, the better.]

Medical definition of rheum: a watery discharge from the mucous membranes especially of the eyes or nose also: a condition [as a cold] marked by such discharge

I use fragments, elements of trash, garbage, disposables, and recyclables. Tiny parts metaphorically remind me of assorted seeds I harvested from my own garden where I planted mother seeds.

The title *rheum* was attached while working on a collage of remnants of paper or cloth and small garbage symbolically representing eye mucus and snot. I remember spending a long time organizing the Michigan school office filing cabinet, removing staples from old documents, and recycling only paper. Rusty staples, corners of paper, and rusty clips linger in my mind, and I can't bear to throw away those trashy things, so I put them in a bag and bring them to the studio, where I sweat and sew with them. I also crochet the throwaway tag ends of vintage yarn into small oval parts to make a large applique piece. Why do I spend all day doing these? My eyes are sore, I sit hunched over, my neck and shoulders ache, and I also have back pain. Why did I choose this kind of life?

Still, there is consolation here. Initially, the studio is a playground. A place for enjoying fresh ideas and new materials. Then, it begins to feel like a prison following boring or bad results. Even if you don't want to be locked up, you choose to stay, to persevere and continue the handiwork, you will have an enlightening experience. Around that time is when dawn seems to shine on the new work, and you can see the light as you exit the tunnel of suffering. Thus, the studio becomes a sanctuary to which we give thanks for enabling us to complete our craft with joy and excitement. Patience is essential.

소소익선 · 쓰레기 재료

소소한 쓰레기로 자투리 종이나 헝겊에 콜라주 작업을 하다가 붙인 제목이rheum이다.

미시간 학교 오피스 서류함을 정리하며 오래된 서류들의 스테이플staple은 떼어내고, 종이만 리사이클 recycle하려 긴 시간을 소모했다. 녹슨 스테이플과 클립clip, 색 바랜 종이 귀퉁이들이 내 마음에 남아 그 쓰레기 같은 물건들을 차마 버리지 못하고 한 자루 담아서 스튜디오에 가져와 그것들로 땀땀이 바느질을 진행했다. 남들은 버릴 자투리 털실로 코바늘뜨기한다고, 그게 뭐라고 온종일을 들일까. 눈도 시고 거북 목이 되어 목과 어깨도 결리고, 또 요통도 도지는데, 나는 왜 이런 삶을 택했나?

그래도 여기에 위안이 있다. 작업실은 처음엔 놀이터이다. 새 아이디어와 재료로 재밌게 노는. 그러다가 지루하고 만족스럽지 않은 결과물에 감옥같이 느껴진다. 그러나 갇혀 있기 싫어도, 튀어 나가지 않고 참고 계속 수작을 하다 보면 깨우치는 순간이 온다. 그럴 즈음에 작업에도 서광이 비쳐 들며 고통의 터널을 빠져나와 빛을 볼 수 있다. 작업실은 마침내 기쁨으로 화하여 감격으로 수작을 할 수 있음에 감사를 드리는 성역이 되는 것이다. 인내가 절실하다.

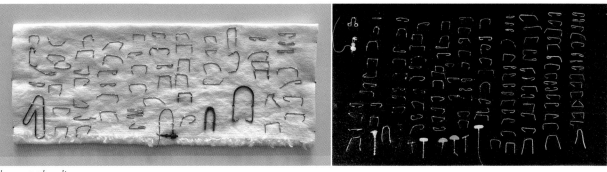

rheum, staples relive

Tag Ends 2021

collecting the insignificant,

stripped to trash,

thrown away, abandoned

to make the time and space of the poems

more open, porous, possible

in the white of a stained blank page,

becoming of things.

something else,

somewhere else.

someone else.

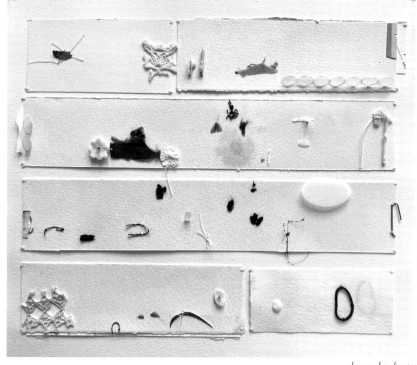

rheum, landscape

work in progress of recycling | 작업실: 실, 구슬, 각종 쇼핑기

January 20, 2023. I'm at Tainan National University of the Arts in Taiwan, engaging in critiques with graduate students and making practical ceramicware in my spare time. The ceramics professor Chang gave me to work with was "stoneware" by Laguna that had a lot of grog [a material usually made from crushed, and ground fired clay] mixed in, imported from California. I had stuck to porcelain since 1995, and while I've made numerous functional ceramicware throughout my career out of necessity, I've only ever shown sculptural works in my exhibitions. This year, I'm planning to produce and exhibit ceramicware using different clay bodies and techniques. Taking a stroll around the sophisticated campus, I was enjoying the abundantly blooming flowers in January, the height of winter, when I received a message from Jihyun in Seoul, saying that Kim Gwangwoo had suddenly died of cancer. I immediately squatted down and gathered three fallen, yellow tropical flowers from the ground in memory of my dear old colleague, but as I tried to say goodbye, my heart collapsed, and I couldn't breathe. I became acquainted with Gwangwoo in 1994, over the four-week summer semester. Back then, I was a graduate student working as an assistant at Alfred University in New York and he was an international student and had just registered for summer school at Alfred. Jihyun and I had recently paid a visit to his Pocheon studio to reunite after some 20 years—I hadn't seen him since the late 1990s—and it had felt as though hardly any time had passed. To think that I can no longer see my colleague of 30 years, who introduced me to The Elegy of Whiteness by Han Kang, who worked with sincerity, whose spirit of non-possession, perseverance, and genuineness inspired me. . . . I had planned to meet up with him once again before returning to the States but had to take a raincheck with this sudden trip to Taiwan. Now, my stomach churns and as I near the verge of a meltdown, forgotten memories come back to me. Why? Why now?

I don't remember much about my early childhood, but there is one incident that I will

작업 노트

2023년 1월 20일 대만, 타이난 국립 미술 대학에 와서 도예과 대학원생들 지도하는 틈틈이, 생활 도기를 만들고 있다. 타이난대 장 선생님이 주신 흙은 캘리포니아 수입산, 라구나Laguna 회사의 그로그 grog가 많이 섞인 회색 석기토이다. 난 1995년부터 백자기토만 써왔고, 도예를 하면서 내가 필요한 그릇을 만들곤 했지만, 전시에 내놓은 적 없이, 조소 위주의 전시를 해왔다. 올해는 그릇을 여러 가지 흙과 다양한 기법으로 만들어 전시도 해보려 하고 있다. 세련된 타이난 대학교 교정을 산책하며 1월 한 겨울인데도 여긴 꽃이 무성하니 참 좋다 하고 있는데, 서울의 지현이에게서 톡이 왔다. 김광우가 암으로 갑자기 세상을 떴다는 전갈이다. 낙화한 노란 열대 꽃 세 송이 모아 놓고 주저앉아, 옛 동무를 기리고 보내려는데, 억장이 무너져 돌아버리겠다. 1994년 대학원 시절에 뉴욕주에 있는 알프레드 학교의 여름학기 조교로 일할 때 알게 된 친구. 90년대 말에 마지막으로 보고 20여 년 만에 지현이와 포천의 작업장에 가서 재회하니, 바로 얼마 전에 보고 헤어진 듯한, 30년 된 옛 동료. 내게 한강 작가의 소설 "흰" 도 소개해 준, 진지하게 작업하는 무소유 속에서 견뎌내는 순수함으로 내게 힘을 주곤 한 친구를 더 이상 볼 수 없다니. 미국으로 가기 전에 꼭 한 번 더 보고 한국을 떠나려 했는데, 갑자기 대만으로 와야 하는 바람에, 다음을 기약했건만... 속이 쓰려 와서 미칠 지경이다. 환장하려니, 끊겼던 필름이, 왜 갑자기?

아주 어릴 적 기억은 별로 없다. 그런 나도 평생 잊지 못하는 어릴 적 일이 있다. 갑자기 내질러진 괴성에, 외할머니도, "이기 먼 소린고?" 하면서 둘러보니 선이 언니가 마당 빨래터에서, 높은 담벼락을 올려보며 외친 절규였다. "선이 언니요, 지두유, 시방, 사람 환장하것슈. 워쩐디유... 미국에 더는 몬 살 거 같애서 한국에 왔는디, 지는 어디로 가야 할지 모르것슈. 옛 친구도 갑자기 죽고, 워쩌유? 환장할랑게 50여 년 전 기억이 불현듯 떠오르나 봐유."

어렴풋한 기억을 더듬어보면, 우리는 종로구 신문로 2가의 본채와 별채가 따로 있는 단층 집에 살았다. 소학교를 갓 마친 충청도 어느 시골 마을의 장녀, 아래로 동생이 예닐곱이나 있다던, 선이 언니가 서울 살이 왔으니... 기껏 열서너 살 어린 소녀였을 텐데, 소녀가장이 되어 남의집살이를, 그것도 서울 한복판, "논두렁도 엄꼬, 아는 사람 아무도 읍는 너므 집에." 주인 내외, 얼라들 넷, 외할머니와 대학 다니던 이모, 여덟 식구가 사는 집에 왔으니, 할머니께서 음식 준비랑 아이들 돌보는 일은 도우셔도, 집안일이 얼마만큼 일지, 한숨...

never forget. One day, my grandmother and I heard a sudden, frustrated scream and looked around to identify the source of the cry, only to find Seoni staring up at the tall wall from the wash place in the yard. It was Seoni. Yes, now that I'm on the verge of a meltdown myself, I understand her. What am I to do? I came to Korea because I couldn't stand to be in America anymore, but now, I can't seem to figure out where I belong. And an old friend died. What do I do? I guess memories from some 50 years ago are suddenly resurfacing now that I'm feeling something similar to what Seoni must have felt back then.

From what I remember, my family lived in a single-story house with a separate annex, on Simunno 2-ga, Jongno-gu. The eldest daughter of a rural family in Chungcheong-do, Seoni had just finished elementary school and had six or seven siblings below her to feed when she came to Seoul to work as a live-in housekeeper at our house. She must have been 13 or 14 at best. Still a young girl, Seoni became the breadwinner of her family and was thrown into the wilderness of Seoul City. There was no rice field, no one she knew and she had to work for a household of eight complete strangers—my father and mother, four children, my grandmother, and my college-student aunt. I can only sigh at the thought of the workload she had to endure—though my grandmother did help out with the cooking and children.

She stayed with my grandmother and aunt in the annex, and I followed her around everywhere, even sharing my 100-won cream bun with her to make her happy. She was like an elder sister to me. My grandmother, Seoni, and I were a trio, and we would go to the market together. I remember Seoni's parents showing up in front of our gate one day with an infant on her mother's back, asking for her. That night, Seoni let out that same losing-her-shit scream again. Imagine the resentment she must have felt right down to the core of her being after her parents dropped by on her payday to take her monthly wage for themselves. I was later told that her younger brother completed high school— and her younger sister, middle school—with Seoni's wage. Wouldn't she have wanted

외할머니와 이모랑 함께 기거하던 별채에 언니도 함께 머물게 되니 나라도 언니한테 위로가 되고 싶어, 100원짜리 크림빵도 나눠 먹고, 나는 언니 옆에 껌딱지였다. 나에겐 제일 맏언니 같은. 할머니랑 해서 우리 3총사가 뭉쳐서 장 보러 함께 가곤 했다. 언니의 부모님이 애기를 들쳐 업고 대문 앞에서 언니를 찾으신 기억. 그날 밤 언니는 또 환장하겠다는 괴성을 질렀다. 그렇게 월급날 오셔서 월급 봉투를 통째로 가져가셨으니 언니는 얼마나 자신의 처지가 원망스러웠을까. 남동생은 중학교, 고등학교까지, 여동생도 중학까지는 언니 월급으로 마쳤다고 들었다. 언니도 힘겹게 번 돈인데. 저금하고 조금은 남겨, 이쁜 머리핀도 사고 가끔은 새 옷도 사고 싶었을 텐데. 여러 해가 지나 내가 국민학교 마치고 중학교에 들어가니, 언니가 영어 알파벳을 가르쳐 달라고도 하고, 내가 연습한 천자문도 달라 했는데, 나중에 보니, 언니는 내가 준 것들로 나름 독학을 하고 있었다. 집에 있던 많은 문학 서적도 읽고, 일기도 쓰고, 자기 계발을 하던 모양이었다. 온종일 집안일하고, 저녁 설거지 마치고 나면, 엄청 피곤했을 텐데. '착할 선[善]' 자가 잘 어울리는 선이 언니.

다시 대만의 오늘로 돌아오니, 난 뭘 그리 환장하겠다니? 환장할 일도 쌨다, 쌨어. 나랑은 비교도 못할 만큼 파란만장한 삶을 산 선이 언니도 있고, 광우는 죽고 없는데. 핑, 왜 핑 자를 쓸까? 눈물이 핑 도니까 나온 질문인데, 이런 건 왜 궁금할까? 광우야, 눈물 받아 담을 그릇도 함 만들어 볼게. 푹 쉬어, 난 철새 되어 여기저기 훨훨 날아볼 텡게.

farewell Gwangwoo, fly away Dongyi

to save her hard-earned money for herself and buy some pretty hairclips or new clothes from time to time? After many years passed and I began attending middle school, Seoni would ask me to teach her the English alphabet and show her the thousands of Chinese characters I practiced writing. I only realized much later that she had taught herself with the materials I gave her, that, after doing all the house chores and dinner dishes, she had read the literature books in our home and written journals at night to better herself. The seon in her name, meaning "goodness" or "virtue," really suited Seoni.

Returning to myself, to today, to Taiwan, as I think about Seoni's wretched life, I realize that I have nothing to melt down over. So, Gwangwoo is dead and gone. "Why do Koreans use the onomatopoeia 'ping' to describe tears welling up around the eyes?" I wonder as I tear up. Why do I even care about that right now? Farewell, Gwangwoo. I'll go and make a vessel for collecting our tears. Rest in peace while I fly around here and there like a migratory bird.

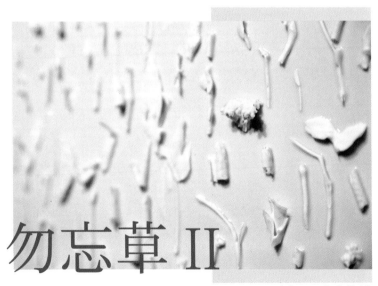

Forget Me Not, exhibition title | 물망초

studio notes [Montana Note]

March 29, 2023. I haven't scribbled in a while. It's been a little over two weeks since I arrived in Montana, and I've been busy unpacking the five boxes of materials from Michigan, soaking and air-drying the parched porcelain clay, kneading clay, and getting started on some new work. I can't remember how long it has been since I last touched clay. I fidgeted with it a little in Switzerland to make rings, but only for about two to three hours a day. Here, I'm working with clay, hands-on, all day and well into the night. I'm currently making a small vase for wild herbs using the coiling and pinching method. It takes me back to the first time I worked with clay when I thought that doing this for the rest of my life would be enough.

The temperature here is still winter cold, around -10°C, but once the sun is out one can hardly sense the cold. The unpaved dirt roads have turned into mire from snow piling, freezing, then melting in the sun. I try to avoid the mire and step on the dry, frozen, or snowy parts of the ground, but from time to time, I end up in a puddle. Sometimes, there's just no way around a mud bath. Thank goodness for my snow boots. The Archie Bray Foundation nestled in a small hill in downtown Helena is a non-profit ceramics institution. This is where I began my artistic career after earning my graduate course degree in 1995, so I've made a full circle in 28 years. What progress the institution has made in the meantime! It has much better facilities now and has also expanded in size. The Residency studio is home to 10 young artists with exceptional talents, and the quantity and volume of the works produced here are as large as the ambitions harbored by the rising artists. Amidst the crowd, I'm working at my own pace and as I need, beginning my studio life anew as I did all those years ago, like the very beginning.

작업 노트[몬타나 노트]

2023년 3월 29일 오랜만에 한마디. 몬타나에 온 지 이 주가 넘어서고 있다. 그동안 바빴다. 미시간에서 보낸 재료 상자 다섯 개 정리. 바싹 마른 자기토, 물에 개어 말리고, 꼬막[흙 반죽] 미는 일, 그리고 새 작업 시작. 얼마 만에 흙을 만지는 건가? 스위스에서 반지 만드느라 흙으로 꼼지락거리긴 하였으나 하루에 두세 시간 정도. 그러나 여기에서는 온종일, 밤 늦게까지, 흙으로 작업하고 있다. 자그마한 들풀 담을 화병을 코일coil과 꼬집기pinching로 올려 가고 있다. '처음처럼,' 맨 처음 흙으로 작업하며, "내 인생은, 이거면 되겠다"라고 했던 그때로.

여기 기온은 아직 한겨울이다. 영하 10도대라고 해도 일단 해가 나면 추운 기운을 감지하지 못한다. 도로가 포장되지 않아 흙길인데 눈이 쌓이고 얼었다가 해가 나면 다 녹아버리니 진탕길이다. 늘 진흙탕을 피해 굳은 땅, 언 땅, 또 눈에 덮인 땅으로 다니다가 어쩌다가 흙탕에 빠질 때가 있다. 흙탕을 피할 길이 없다. 눈 장화를 신었으니 망정이지. 낮은 동산에 둘러싸인 '아치 브레이 파운데이션Archie Bray Foundation,' 헬레나Helena 시내에 자리잡은 비영리 도예기관이다. 내가 1995년에 대학원을 마치고 처음으로 미술 일을 시작한 곳에 28년 만에 다시 온 것이다. 그동안 시설이 엄청 좋아지고 규모도 커졌다. 괄목상대! 뛰어난 젊은 작가 열 명이 모여 있는 곳이다. 큰 야망을 품은 젊은이들이 빚어내는 작품이니만큼, 그 양과 크기가 압도적이다. 그 와중에 나는 나의 필요와 속도에 맞춰 나의 스튜디오 생활을 '처음처럼' 열어 가고 있다.

Montana Sky Montana is known as Big Sky State

WONDER LUST

방랑벽

loss. being lost. nobody.

From here, I live over there. I'm not certain if I don't like being here or simply long to be there. Over there, I long to come back here. Between here and there, I am indeed forever lost. Belonging nowhere, neither America, nor Korea, I realize that the only place I belong to is the studio, wherever it is. Therefore, I keep my hands busy working in the studio or think about working even when my hands are at rest. This way, I feel safe and have a sense of being and belonging.

If you look at famous artists in books or magazines, you can recognize that they have exhibited the same type of work for several decades. Most of my teachers also maintain one body of work for an extended period of time. I also thought that the *Immigrant Flowers* series, which I did around the time I graduated from graduate school, was the work that I could continue making for the next 30–40 years. After graduate school, I went to the Archie Bray Foundation residency in Montana, taught part-time at the University of Washington in Seattle, and worked at the Anderson Ranch Art Center residency in Colorado, dedicating myself to working as an almost full-time artist. Coincidentally, the work was received favorably, invited to many exhibitions, sold, and it appeared in magazines. It became a well-known work. But then, at the Europees Keramisch Werkcentrum [EKWC] residency in the Netherlands, I was introduced to the French porcelain Limoges, which was completely different from the porcelain I usually used. As I became more curious about the environment that surrounded me, I wondered what it would be like to physically embed this new experience and journey into my work. Again, after some time, when I went to China to work with Jingdezhen porcelain, I was curious as to what kind of work could only be done in Jingdezhen, so I tried my hand at creating large porcelain tiles. Trying something new is exciting at first, but you soon discover that the new work is pretty bad. It's so embarrassing that you want to stop. You're lost for a long time. Still, if you keep at it, you're sure to find something. That's the visual clarity I find. Then, when

상실하여. 잃어버린. 아무도 아닌.

여기에서, 나는 거기에 살고 있다. 내가 여기 있기를 싫어하는지, 아니면 거기에 있기를 원하는지 확신하지 못한다. 거기에 가면 이곳에 다시 오려 한다. 여기와 거기 사이에서, 나는 나를 잃어버린다. 나는 미국이나 한국에 속하지 않고, 내가 속한 유일한 곳이 스튜디오라는 것을 깨닫는다, 그게 어디든. 그래서 나는 스튜디오에서 일하는 동안 손을 바쁘게 움직이거나 손이 쉴 때에도 작업 생각을 한다. 이 방법으로, 나는 나의 존재와 소속에 대해 안도감을 느낀다.

책이나 잡지에서 유명 미술 작가들을 보면 몇십 년 동안 한 종류의 작품을 전시하더라. 나의 선생님들도 거의 한 가지 작업 세계를 유지하신다. 나도 대학원을 졸업할 즈음 시작한 "이화" 시리즈가 나의 작업이고 한 30~40년 해도 되는 줄 알았다. 몬타나의 아치 브레이 레지던시에 가서, 시애틀의 워싱턴 대학교 강사 시절, 그리고 콜로라도의 앤더슨 랜치 레지던시에서 거의 전업 작가처럼 열심을 다했다. 마침 호감을 갖고 봐주고 불러 주는 전시도 여럿 잡히고, 팔리기도 하며 값도 올라가고, 잡지에도 나고, 나름 알려지는 작품이 되었는데, 돌연 네덜란드의 EKWC 레지던시로 가는 바람에 새로운 작업 세계로, 곁길로 샜다. 네덜란드에서 쓰는 프랑스 흙, 리모주Limoges 자기토의 감촉은 내 자기토와 전혀 다르고 그 새로운 세상에서 보고 겪는 새로운 인생길에선 새 경험을 작업으로 옮기면 어떨까 싶어서. 궁금했기 때문에. 또 한참 후 징더전Jingdezhen[경덕진, 景德鎭] 자기토 작업하러 중국에 갔을 땐, 또 징더전에서만 할 수 있을 작업은 어떤 건지 궁금해서 큰 도판 작업을 새로 시도하고. 새로운 시도는 처음엔 재밌지만 곧 후지다는 걸 알게 된다. 쪽팔려서 접어 버리고 싶다. 상당 기간 헤맨다. 그래도 계속하면 뭔가 보인다. 그건 내가 발견하게 되는 시각적 명료함이다. 그러다 한 작업군이 궤도에 올라서면 난 또 다른 옆길로 샌다. 바늘을 늘 흙 도구로 쓰니 직접 바느질을 하면 어떨까? 나만의 바느질 작업은 뭐가 될까? 그러니 흙 작업 외에도 종이에, 헝겊에 바늘을 사용한다.

나는 내가 하고 싶은 작업을 하려고. 궁금증을 풀려고, 나만이 발견해야 하는 수작품이 어딘가에서 날 기다리고 있어서, 길을 또 떠난다. 그런데 이 서로 다른 듯한 작업군은 따지고 보면 같은 콘셉트concept 아래 한가족이다. 큰길에서 뻗어 나와 결국 서로 통하는 샛길.

69

one body of work is on track, I escape into another side street of enquiry. Needles are always used as clay tools, so why not include actual needlework on fabric? What would my personal style of needlework look like? So, in addition to working with clay, I attempt taking needles to paper and cloth.

I set out on the road again to create what I wanted to create, to discover the answers to my curiosity, and to meet the handcrafts that were waiting somewhere just for me. However, these seemingly disparate series of work are in fact a single family under the same concept. The side road that extends away from the main road eventually circles back and connects to it again.

Feeling like Grass Blades
"The petals fall in the wind endlessly
There is no promise of the day we meet
why can't our hearts get connected?
Only blades of grass get tied."

"While walking along the path in the barley fields,
there is a voice calling that stopped my walk.
When I look back, I see no one
only evening sunset, only the empty sky
catches my eye."

채근담[菜根譚]에서
정중동[靜中動]은 고요할 정, 가운데 중, 움직일 동의 한자
고요할 정 가운데 중 움직일 동이라 고요함 속에 떨림과 움직임, 가녀린 흔들림

달 나오고, 꽃은 지고.
설리춘색[雪裏春色], 눈 밑에 이미 봄이 와 있다. 차디차게 새하얀 배꽃 봉오리 안에, 희고도 찬 보름달
뒷면에도 갖가지 색깔이 머금어 있지 아니허냐? 그 빛깔을 길어 오르는 일이 내게 주어져 시나브로
한 빛깔, 또 한 빛깔 드러냄이 내 숙명이려니 한다. 하여, 처량한 달밤에, 불현듯, "첫날밤에 달 보고
울었드래요." 따로 된 갑순이와 갑돌이의 어긋난 사랑 노랫말이 갑자기 튀어나오니, 이어서 떠오르는 노래
가사들.

"보리밭 사잇길로 걸어가면 뉘 부르는 소리 있어 발을 멈춘다.
돌아보면 아무도 보이지 않고 저녁노을 빈 하늘만 눈에 차누나."

"오가며 그 집 앞을 지나노라면 그리워 나도 몰래 발이 머물고 오히려 눈에 띌까 다시 걸어도
되오면 그 자리에 서졌습니다."

"꽃잎은 하염없이 바람에 지고, 만날 날은 아득타,
기약이 없네. 무어라 맘과 맘은 맺지 못하고,
한갓되이 풀잎만 맺으려는고, 한갓되이 풀잎만
맺으려는고."

정관사 [Definite Article: the]와 부정관사 [Indefinite Article: a/an]
Syntax: combination of words into sentences

Studying Foreign languages

Qui êtes-vous?
C'est Moi.
그것은 나입니다.
It is me.
这是我。

March 2, 2023. When I first visited Switzerland in 2018, I began studying French in the hopes that I would settle there, only to give up after just two days. Now, I find myself wanting to settle in Switzerland again after experiencing how hard life in Korea can be, but with my memory increasingly failing me, how am I to handle all the memorization and learning a new language entails? I still struggle with English grammar, especially with definite articles, and even Korean grammar, with final consonants and spacing. Never mind the fact that I've already forgotten anything that I had learned of Chinese.

Buyu in Korean can mean both "drifting about" and "rich" depending on the combination of Chinese characters. When I use the word buyu, I mean that I'm adrift, not rich. It's at times like these that the Chinese characters I learned come in handy. In any case, I intend to *buyu* [浮遊, drift about] and die *buyu* [富裕, rich]—at least at heart.

수평선 상의 문법

정관사[Definite Article: the]와 부정관사
[Indefinite Article: a/an]
Syntax: the combination of words into sentences

Studying Foreign languages

Qui êtes-vous?
C'est Moi.
그것은 나입니다.
It is me.
这是我。

2023년 3월 2일 스위스에 처음 온 2018년, 스위스에
정착하고 싶은 마음에, 불어 공부를 시작했으나, 좀
해보다가 이틀 만에 집어치웠다. 한국살이 힘드니,
이번에도 여기에서 살고 싶은 마음이나, 점점 심해지는
건망증으로 암기를 어찌 감당하냐고? 영어도 문법,
특히 정관사, 한국어는 받침, 띄어쓰기가 엉망이고,
중국어 배운 건 벌써 다 까먹어 버렸는데.

부유하다. 부자가 아니고 떠돈다고요. 그래서 한자
[漢字]가 필요해. 浮遊, 떠돌이로 살다가 마음이나 富
裕하게, 숨을 거둘 요량이다.

Connecting Dots II, Funeral Nights, exhibition views

ARCHIVE |
COLLECTION OF WORK

모듬: 작

GodeLee: Connecting Dots

Between Lausanne and East Lansing,
4222 mils [6799 km] away

I met Sylvie Godel in 2010. We crossed paths while engaging in separate explorations in Jingdezhen porcelain in China. We sensed many common threads in our artistic endeavors, especially "white on white" aesthetics, so we talked about connecting the creative dots of our ideas. Since 2011, we have collaborated in East Lansing, Michigan, and Lausanne, Switzerland, creating a series of slip-cast functional ware and sculptural objects. We named our collaboration team GodeLee by combining our family names. In Lausanne in 2023, we once again gathered our creative forces, processes, and material explorations for the exhibition titled *Connecting Dots II*.

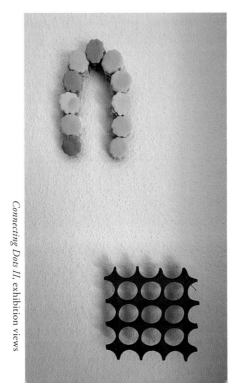

Connecting Dots II, exhibition views

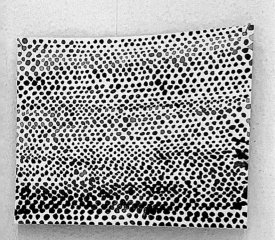

고델리 · 로잔 · 이스트 랜싱

2010년에 실비 고델Sylvie Godel을 만났다. 중국에서
징더전 자기토로 각자 실험을 하는 동안 여정이
교차되었다. 우리는 서로의 예술적 시도에서 많은
공통점을 찾았다. 특히 백색의 미학으로 우리의 창작
아이디어를 함께 모아 보기로 합의를 보았다. 2011
년부터 미시간주의 이스트 랜싱East Lansing과 스위스
로잔Lausanne에서 협력하여 일련의 슬립 주입법slip
casting으로 그릇 및 조각품을 제작했다. 우리는 우리의
성[姓]을 결합하여 팀 이름을 'GodeLee'로 명했다. 다시
2023년 3월, 로잔에서, 우리는 작업도 같이 하고 재료에
대한 연구도 같이 진행하여 팀 전시회, Connecting
Dots II를 열었다.

GodeLee: between Lausanne and East Lansing

We draw a Venn diagram to list our similarities. Our common interests include visiting antique shops, cemeteries, and libraries as well as looking at the still life paintings of Giorgio Morandi, among others. We both pay attention to that which is overlooked, the trivial. We discussed what project to pursue within the short two-week period spent visiting each other's studios. For GodeLee collaborations, four hands work on the same objects. We don't talk much once we begin the production phase. We communicate visually, instinctively know what to do, and move accordingly. We work quickly. We think a lot about why we make each piece. Why? As if. Because. . . . As Maya Lin said, "I think with my hands." We find answers as our hands become busy.

GodeLee table sets

고델리 · 로잔 · 이스트 랜싱

우리는 우리의 유사성을 찾기 위해 벤다이어그램 차트를 그린다. 우리의 공통된 관심사는 골동품 가게, 묘지, 도서관을 방문하는 것과 조르조 모란디Giorgio Morandi의 정물화 감상이다. 우리는 무의미한 것과 무시된 것에 관심을 보이는 공통점이 있다. 우리는 서로의 스튜디오에서 2주간의 짧은 방문 기간 내에 어떤 프로젝트를 추진할지 논의한다. GedeLee 공동작업을 위해, 손 넷이 동일한 물건을 만드는 데 함께 한다. 우리는 작업 단계에선 많은 이야기를 하지 않고, 시각적으로 의사 소통을 하고 각 단계에서 무엇을 해야 하는지 눈치채면, 그에 따라 협업한다. 우리는 엄청 빠르게 일한다. 우리는 무엇을 왜 만드는지에 대해 골똘히 생각한다. 왜 하는가? 왜냐하면... "나는 손으로 생각한다"던 마야 린Maya Lin 의 말처럼, 우리 질문의 답도 손이 바빠질 때 찾아진다.

GodeLee Homage to Morandi

CARE. not convenience.

To the earth, the sky, and the sea,

the flowers' heart, the clouds' greetings, the waves' courage.

With the utmost kindness and sincerity,

let us console the Earth and connect, heart to heart.

CARE. not convenience., exhibition posters

I pay attention to my natural surroundings and contemplate various plant elements in my work. The main inspiration comes from nature in general, my own garden in Michigan, and memories of my mom's garden in Seoul. Gardens with a variety of flowering plants serve as metaphorical homes to return to and lead to the development of my own visual interpretation, one that is personal, yet abstract. I am interested in applying this interpretation as a means of conveying the inner landscape of the heart and mind. I aim to demonstrate a deep sense of responsibility and concern for the environment, which runs throughout my creative practice and teaching, while also serving the university and the community. I am pushing the boundaries of communication with my experimentation in artistic intention, materiality, and production. While upcycling recyclables and

보살핌. 편리함이 아니라.

대지에게, 하늘에게, 바다에게
꽃이 오는 마음, 구름이 전하는 인사, 파도가 주는 용기
따스한 친절과 다정한 진심으로
우리 모두를 달래, 마음과 마음을 이어가

나는 자연 풍광과 다양한 식물성 요소들에 주의를 기울인다. 나는 자연에서 주로 영감을 받는데, 미시간에 있는 내 정원과 내 기억 속 서울 집에 있던 어머니의 정원이 특히 영감을 준다. 갖가지 꽃이 피는 정원들은 돌아가고 싶은 집과 같아 나만의 시각적 해석, 개인적이고도 추상적인 해석을 전개하게 하고, 이 해석을 이용해 마음속 내면 풍경을 전달하는 것이 중요하다. 나의 목표는 환경에 대한 깊은 책임감과 우려를 표현하는 것으로 내 창작 과정, 강의, 그리고 대학 기관과 지역사회를 위한 활동 전체를 관통한다. 나는 또한 예술적 의도, 구체성, 그리고 제작과 관련된 실험을 통해 소통의 한계를 탈피하는 중이다. 재활용품을 업사이클링하여 종이 위에 콜라주한 *rheum* 시리즈를 만들면서 나는 시각적 소통이 폭넓은 사회적 변화에 도달하는 강력한 수단이라는 믿음을 갖게 되었고, 그 믿음은 나를 명상적 성소와도 같은 스튜디오에서 벗어나 사람들에게 행동을 촉구하도록 이끌었다. 나는 미시간 주립 대학교에서 켈리 맥아더Kelly MacArthur 그래픽디자인 교수, 지역사회 지속가능성부의 리씨 고랄닉Lissy Goralnik 교수와 팀을 이뤄 지역사회 프로젝트 CARE. not convenience.를 위해 여러 가지 일을 함께 했다. 우리가 수집한 비닐봉지들을 이용해 내가 예술적 조형물로 만드는 동안 동료들은 그래픽디자인과 연구, 지역사회를 기반으로 하는 워크숍workshop을 준비했다. 이 창조적 협동의 초점은 예술과 디자인 설치 작업에 비닐봉지를 활용함으로써 참가자들이 상호적 관계 속에서 폐품을 가치 있는 공동 창작품으로 변모시키도록 하는 것이었다. 학생들과 교수들, 직원들과 지역사회는 '비닐 파티'와 같은 행사, 워크숍과 강연, 설치작품들을 통해 환경을 위한 활동과 연결된다. 그러한 활동들은 우리 지역사회와 미시간 주립 대학교는 물론 펜실베이니아 주립 대학교, 오리건 주립 대학교, 나아가 아이오와주의 마하리시 국제대학교 등 캠퍼스에서 펼쳐졌다.

81

bits of trash into collage works on paper for the rheum series, my belief in visual communication as a powerful tool that enacts broad social change, urged me to step out of the contemplative sanctuary of my studio to reach out and move people to action. To that end, I teamed up with two MSU professors, Kelly Salchow MacArthur in Graphic Design and Lissy Goralnik in Community Sustainability, to collaborate on community-engaged projects and an art exhibition, CARE. not convenience. We were engaged in all facets of the project, but I was in charge of turning collected plastic bags into art forms while other colleagues engaged in graphic design as well as research and community-based workshops. The focus of this creative collaboration was to use plastic bags as the material for art and design installations, thereby offering an interactive and engaging way for participants to transform waste into a collaborative, creative work with value. A community making event ["plastic party"], workshops, lectures, and art installations connect the students, faculty, staff, and community, with environmental action. The project took place at various locations on campus, within the local community, and went beyond MSU campus to reach Pennsylvania State University, Oregon State University, and Maharishi International University in Iowa.

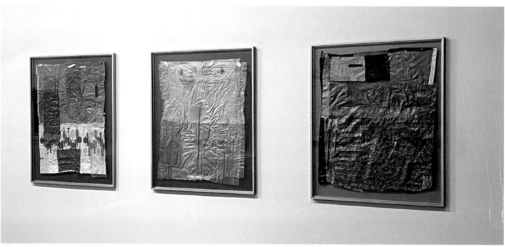

after shopping, recycled plastic shopping bags

CARE. not convenience. exhibition view

CARE. not convenience.

"Our collaborative work aspired to shed light on society's dependence and careless overuse as well as thoughtless disposal of plastic. Throughout our collaboration, found and collected plastic bags have been the primary material used for creating works. By choosing to work with this ubiquitous, worthless material, we created value by repurposing and upcycling plastic through textual, graphic design, and art-making methods. We are committed to eliminating waste through our creative process. The extensive exploration of this petroleum-based material has led to methods of fusing sheets of plastic with heat, and making art forms with functional design capabilities, such as wearable art, bags, and hanging space dividers."

—from the collaborators' statement

vinyl wearables

보살핌. 편리함이 아니라

"우리의 협업은 사회의 플라스틱 의존성과 플라스틱의 과도한 사용, 그리고 플라스틱의 무분별한 폐기와 같은 암울한 현실을 조명하고자 한다. 우리의 작업에 사용할 주요 재료로 재활용이 중단되어 버려질 플라스틱 봉투들을 수집했다. 어디에서나 볼 수 있는 이 무가치한 재료를 우리는 텍스트text, 그래픽 디자인graphic design 및 예술 창작 방법을 적용해 용도를 새롭게 부여하고 업사이클링upcycling 함으로써 새로운 가치를 창출한다. 이 석유화학산업의 소산물인 플라스틱 봉투를 잘라 실처럼 만들어 뜨개질 및 직조에 사용할 뿐만 아니라 낮은 열을 가해 플라스틱 시트sheet를 만들어 여기에 재봉질을 하여 몸에 착용하거나 들고 다닐 수 있는 가방이나 거실 공간을 나누는 시트 등 기능성 미술품을 만들 수도 있고, 화랑의 설치 전시에도 활용할 수 있을 것이다. 우리의 작업 과정으로 인한 쓰레기가 더 이상 나오지 않도록 한다."

의도문에서

CARE. not convenience. exhibition view. recycled vinyl banners

Immigrant Flowers

In the background of the *Immigrant Flowers* series, I reflect on objects like books, lunch boxes, handkerchiefs as well as meanings of embroidery, wrapping cloths, and threads. A book held in one's hands. The first thought that comes to mind is the feeling of a book's weight when held in both hands. Next is the book design, especially its cover. Font choice comes after that. Ironically, the impact and influence that a book had on me is probably only my fifth or sixth reason for liking books. As I spend time thinking on books, I reminisce about my college-student aunt and grandmother. They both lived with my family and my grandma helped to take care of house chores and the four children. At night, my grandmother did needlework or embroidered small flowers onto the corners of her white hankies, as her daughter sat next to her, reading. Grandma used to hand a lunch box wrapped in the flower-embroidered hanky to my mom who was going to work. My grandfather died long before I was born. During the Korean War, my grandma lost my mother's older brother and sister. My grandma's eyes were always wet with clear water. I learned what a widow was through grandma. Now as I think of her perpetually sad eyes, I wonder if she used the flower-embroidered hanky when she wiped her tears away. My aunt used to read a book to me at my bedside. Only now I recall the memory of falling asleep with teary eyes over hermit Jean Valjean's misery. My beautiful, calm, and intelligent aunt was grandmother's youngest child. My mom was always busy with her teaching job, so I was closer to my grandma and my aunt who lived in the guest house next to the main house where my parents and three siblings lived. When did they move away? Around the time I started grade school?

Aunt Park Mu-og [Abundant Jade], more commonly goes by Hae-jung. I heard later that she led a forlorn life. Back then, nobody talked to me about my revered aunt's untimely death. Now, at this age of mine, I understand why. . . .

이화[離花]

이화[離花] 시리즈의 배경엔, 책, 도시락통, 손수건과 같은 물건과, 바느질, 보자기, 그리고 실에 대한 사유가 있다. 책이 주는 묵직함, 손안에. 책이 좋은 이유를 들자니 처음 머릿속에 드는 생각은, 두 손 안에 느껴지는 책의 무게다. 그다음이 책 디자인, 특히 겉표지. 글자체font 고르기에 무지 까다로운 나에겐, 책이 좋은 이유를 순위대로 꼽으라 하면, 책의 내용은 아마도 대여섯 번째쯤? 책 하면 또 넷이나 되는 손주들을 돌보시느라 함께 사시던 외할머니와 대학 다니던 이모 생각. 밤이 되면 책 읽는 이모 곁에서 바느질하시던 할머니. 손수건 귀퉁이에 수도 놓던. 할머닌 꽃수 놓은 수건에 도시락 통을 싸 출근하시던 엄마에게 건네주셨다. 내가 태어나기도 전에 돌아가셨다는 외할아버지. 6·25 때 잃은, 엄마보다 손위의 두 삼촌들과 이모 하나. 늘 투명한 물기로 촉촉하던 할머니 두 눈, 지금도 기억에 선하다. 과부가 어떤 사람을 일컫는지도 일찌감치 알게 해 준 할머닌 꽃수 놓인 손수건으로 눈물도 훔치셨을까? 이모는 내 머리맡에서 책을 읽어 주곤 했다. 장 발장의 억울함에 뿌예지던 눈으로 잠이 든 기억이 지금에야 돌아오니, 무옥이 이모. 참 아름답고 차분하고 지적인 할머니 막내딸. 엄마는 국어 교사로 늘 바쁘시니, 나는 부모님과 세 형제가 사는 집 옆의 별채에 사시던 할머니하고 이모와 더 가까웠다. 그들이 이사 나가신 때는, 내가 국민학교에 입학했을 때였던가?

박무옥[朴戊玉] 이모. 혜정이란 이름으로 더 자주 불리던. 내가 우러르던 이모는 불행한 삶을 사시다가 요절하셨다는데, 아무도 이모 얘기를 해주지 않아 애가 타던 기억. 이젠 이 나이에 그냥 알아지네...

"The objects she makes are the metaphorical reductive crucibles of her inner literary world. Thrust into the heart of American culture after the relative insulation of her secluded family life, Jae Won Lee's immersion was an acute life change, so alarming that the term 'homesickness' only begins to describe the cultural alienation she experienced upon her arrival. Her reaction, her contemplative stoic introspection, would ultimately become her focus, sanctuary, and default position.

"In losing her voice, in turning inward, Jae Won Lee eventually developed a new voice. Part of this voice is its reductive vocabulary, and intrinsic to the vocabulary is the use of the ellipse, which finds its origin in the waning and waxing of the moon."

—from *Internal Distance[s]*, by Dick Goody

Crochet Medley, vintage yarn, 2021–23

Immigrant Flowers

Clay allows me a personal language. I write a journal as an act of faith, recording the attentions of the moment. When the language I use is exclusively visual, my journal becomes a sequence of small ceramic containers. I have worked to evoke something elusive by reducing the forms to their ultimate necessities. The tendency toward reductivism regarding forms reinforces their mystery. These objects are a synthesis of minimal sentences and enigmatic silences. I desire a certain tension between clarity and ambiguity. I want my message in its empathy, simplicity, and sensitivity to evoke a sense of isolation. The viewer remains a spectator.

The sealed porcelain box forms appear unitary, simple, and introverted; however, the surface treatment reveals subtle complexities and allusions in an elaborate and exuberant way. Through the floral patterns on the surface, I seek to manifest the inner dialogue surrounding gender and ethnicity that is becoming increasingly central to my evolving from a Korean to a Korean-American female artist. I am an observer of cross-cultural confrontation. I am interested in the simple expression of complex thoughts.

As if using colorful threads and a needle to embroider flowers, I inlay [special technique] floral motifs on the surface of porcelain box forms using colored porcelain slips. The sculptures' forms are reminiscent of lunch boxes or books, ranging from a small poetry book to novels and large picture books. There is hollow space within each sealed box form, a small and intimate space—this is all I could demand as my own space.

A poetic investigation of floral patterns prevails in my work. The images on the porcelain tiles hint at the flowering plants of an ethereal garden, emerging from memories of my childhood. I am particularly interested in floral patterns for their characteristics of self-generation, repetition, and balance. Constant questions arise as I attempt to reach beyond the surface concerns of visual inquiry and instead touch on profound insights through reductive expression and condensed visuals. I explore the divisions and unifications of nature, culture, and society.

이화[離花]

흙은 내게 개인적 언어를 허용한다. 나는 순간을 기록하는 믿음의 행위로 글을 쓴다. 나의 언어가 전적으로 시각적일 때, 나의 글은 작은 도자 합[盒, 상자] 시리즈가 된다. 나는 간단 명료한 합의 형태에 오히려 애매모호함을 불러일으키고자 했다. 최소로 줄인 합 형태의 축약성은 상자에 신비함을 더한다. 이 합[盒]들은 최소의 문장과 알 수 없는 침묵의 합[盒]인 것이다. 나는 명확성과 불확실성의 사이, 다소의 긴장감을 추구한다. 내 메시지가 공감, 간결함, 섬세함으로 고립의 느낌을 불러 일으키기를 원한다. 보는 이는 여전히 관객일 뿐.

닫힌 백자토 합은 단순하고 내성적인 듯 보이나 정교하고 활기찬 표면 처리는 미묘한 복잡성을 제시한다. 표면의 패턴을 통해 나는 성별과 민족에 관한 내면의 대화를 유도하고, 이는 내가 한국인에서 한-미 여성 예술가로 변화하는 데 더 중점을 두고 있다. 나는 비교문화라는 현상에 직면하는 관찰자이다. 나는 사려 깊은 생각을 단순하게 표현하는 데 관심이 있다.

색실 펜 바늘로 꽃수를 놓는 것처럼, 나는 상감 기법으로 바늘로 백자기토의 흙 상자 겉 표면에 꽃 문양을 새겨 넣는다. 합은 도시락과 책, 시집부터, 소설책, 큰 사진 책 같은 것들을 연상시키는데, 봉인된 상자 형태 안에 빈 공간이 있다. 그 작은, 은밀한 공간은 내가 요구할 수 있는 나만의 유일한 곳이다.

꽃 패턴에 대한 詩的 탐구는 나의 작품에 만연하다. 백자토 합의 이미지는 어린 시절의 추억 속 정원의 꽃식물에서 온다. 나는 특히 꽃 패턴의 자기 생성, 반복성 및 균형에 관심이 있다. 시각적 탐구의 표면적 배려를 넘어, 함축적인 표현과 시각적인 압축을 통한 깊은 통찰력을 목표로 하면서 끊임없이 질문을 제기한다. 나는 자연, 문화 및 사회의 분열과 통합을 모색한다.

handkerchief | 손수건 재생

실絲,

실로 작업하며 시선, 눈길에 대한 생각이 많다.

시선視線은 눈이 가는 길. 관심을 이르는 단어인데, 눈길은 어떤한 곳이나 일, 어떤 사람. 물건에 머물러서 관심을 기울이게 한다.

무심히 바라보다가 눈길을 떼지 못하는 물건, 고개를 돌려도 관심을 거두지 못하는 사람이 있다.

실은 길이, 거리 및 연결되는 만남을 의미한다.

Thread. I think about the concepts of eyesight and gaze as I work with thread. A line of sight refers to the path that eyes naturally follow. It is a word that extends interest, by glancing at a certain place, object, or someone. It draws attention to something. Even when gazing indifferently, there are certain things that you can't take your eyes off of. Likewise, there are people you can't take your attention away from even if you turn your head. Threads indicate length, distance, and the connection between encounters.

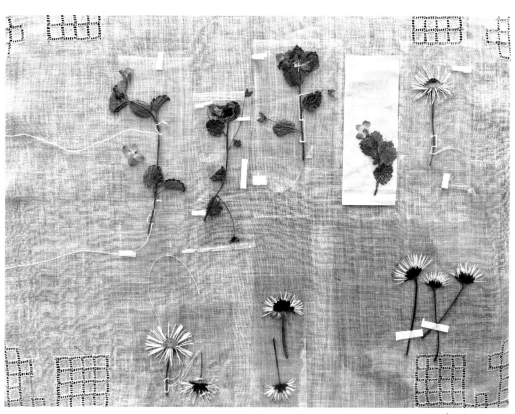

Between Pages │ 책갈피 사이

And about Books

What am I doing writing and making a book instead of an Instagram account in this digital age? I'm part of what people call the "in-between generation," the baby boomers caught between the analog and digital eras, who understand the power of Instagram, yet can't quite get themselves involved because of pride, self-esteem issues, or digital illiteracy. Before I knew it, I had become an oldie, catching myself flinching at words like *kkondae* [condescending superior] or "nosy." I'm at an age where I need to watch what I say and think. Even though I'm sensitive to others acting like *kkondae*, I don't pay attention to my own words and often catch myself uttering the condescending equivalent of "Back in my days. . . ."

Anyhow, I've always been keenly aware of the importance of books and the agony experienced by those who write them. I can easily surmise how painstaking the process of filling in blank pages with words is. Hence, every time I open up a book, I am humbled by the private encounter with the author and admire the arduous form of white-collar labor. Texts printed in black ink had a larger influence on the way I think than any one person or empirical experience. Throughout my childhood and youth, I encountered the world—both East and West, ancient and modern—through books. I would carry them around in my arms and sometimes use them as pillows to take fast naps and these memories always bring warmth to my heart. I remember owning the World Literature series published by Eulyumungo with light khaki covers. I wonder where they went and when. Both my parents and I have traveled so much, to different countries and cities, and the belongings we've had to let go of in the process continue to haunt me with regret.

When I was little, I thought of becoming an ethics teacher or a counselor, but above all, I wanted to become a poet—a far reach I never realized. Still, I wonder why I liked ethics as a subject. I also liked learning the Chinese Thousand-Character Classic. When kids

그리고 책에 대하여

디지털 시대에 인스타나 시작하지, '먼' 글을 쓰고, '먼' 책을 만든다니? '낀 세대'라고 한단다. 인스타의 효력을 알지만, 자존심, 자존감 때문에, 혹 컴맹이라 능력이 안 되는 아날로그와 디지털 시대 사이에 낀 베이비 붐baby boom 세대에 속한 사람들. 어느새 쉰 세대에 속해, 꼰대, 오지랖 같은 단어를 듣게 되면 '쫌' 움칠하게 된다. 입단속, 마음 조심. 남의 꼰대질에 민감하나 스스로의 "나는 말이야, 우리 때는 말이지..." 같은 언사에는 무딜 수 있다.

여하튼, 책의 의미. 글 쓰는 이들의 고충은 진작부터 알고 있었다. 하얀 빈 공간에 단어를 채워 넣는 글 쓰는 과정의 고통은 지레짐작이 되었다. 책 읽는 순간, 글쓴이를 독대하는 겸허한 순간이고 그의 화이트 칼라 중노동에 대한 존경의 경험이다. 검정 잉크로 인쇄된 글은 나의 사고 체계에 큰 영향을 주었다. 그 어떤 사람이나 실제 인생 경험보다 앞선다.

95

Spring Rain, detail

who disliked it asked me why I liked it, I would say, "Just because!" As it turned out, though, there was no such thing as a teacher who only teaches ethics. My first choice for a major was education, but I didn't make the score cut. My second choice was psychology, which I thought would give me insight into the human mind and offer some consolation after being degraded as a second-rate person all as the result of a test that took place over a single day. Then, after multiple twists and turns, I've ended up working with my hands and visual language, the writing-like process of which is therapeutic for someone like me who was never good enough at speaking or writing. Stitch by stitch, I continue to imitate writing with my needle, searching for the perfect metaphor. I hope my artworks read like a book.

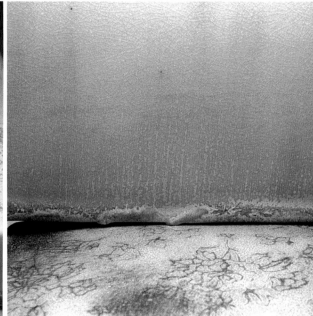

At Parting

Taste of Lime, detail

유년 시절, 청소년 시절, 동서고금을 책 속에서 만나며, 책을 끼고, 때로는 책을 베개 삼아 오수에 곤히 떨어지기도 하던 추억은 마음에 흐뭇함을 가져온다. 을유문고에서 출간한 세계문학전집은 은은한 카키 khaki색으로 기억되는데. 그 전집은 언제, 어디에서 소실되었을까? 부모님도, 나도, 여러 나라, 여러 도시로 옮겨 다니느라 포기한 물건들, 후에 마음이 착잡해지는 순간이 허다하다.

어려서 장래 소망은 바른생활 교사, 상담사, 로망[이루지 못할]은 시인. 쾅. 근데 왜 바른생활 과목이 좋았는지는 아직도 잘 모르겠음. 나는 천자문[天字文]을 배우는 것도 좋아했는데, 한자 공부를 싫어하던 친구들의 "왜"라는 질문에 내 대답은 "그냥, 그냥 좋은데!". 바른생활 교사가 될 수 있는 전공은 따로 없다고 해서, 1차[1류] 대학 지원은 교육학과로. 그러나 불합격. 사람의 마음을 알아 갈 수 있을 것 같아, 특히 하루에 친 대입시험 결과로 당장, 2차, 2류 인생으로 전락하는 마음의 상처를 위로할 수도 있으려니 심리학이 딱일 것 같았다. 그러다 여차저차 끝에 시각의 언어로 손작업에 몰두하는 사람이 되어 말재주, 글재주 딸리니, 글을 써 내려가듯 하는 작업 과정을 통해 스스로 치유 중이다. 시구[詩句]를 찾듯이 한 땀씩 바늘로 써 내려간다. 책 같은 미술작업이 되면 좋겠다.

97

Immigrant Flowers, exhibition view

And about Books: Power of printed words

"We read to know we are not alone."

—T. S. Lewis

"Distance was a dangerous thing, she knew. Distance changed people. Look at her own case—she could never return now to live with her family in the city."

"But nobody ever forgot anything, not really, though sometimes they pretended, when it suited them. Memories were permanent. . . . Remembering bred its own peculiar sorrow. It seemed so unfair; that time should render both sadness and happiness into a source of pain."

—from *A Fine Balance* by Rohinton Mistry

"It's been a tough century for modesty, craftsmanship and tenderness. . . . Making art can feel dangerous and revealing. . . . Making art precipitates self-doubt, stirring deep waters that lay between what you know you should be, and what you fear you might be."

—from *Art & Fear: Observations on the Perils [and Rewards] of Artmaking* by David Bayles

"Surely all art is the result of one's having been in danger, of having gone through an experience all the way to the end, where no one can go any further. The further one goes, the more private, the more personal, the more singular an experience becomes, and the thing one is making is, finally, the necessary, irrepressible, and as nearly as possible, the definitive utterance of this singularity."

—from *Letters to a Young Poet* by Rainer Maria Rilke

그리고 책에 대하여:
인쇄된 검은 글자의 능력

"이 낯선 도시에서 왜 자꾸만 오래된
기억들이 떠오르는 걸까?
. . . 내가 겪어온 삶의 모든 기억들이,
그 기억들과 분리해낼 수 없는 내
모국어와 함께 고립되고 봉인된 것처럼
느껴진다. 고립이 완고해질수록 뜻밖의
기억들이 생생해진다. 지난 여름 내가
도망치듯 찾아든 곳이 지구 반대편의
어떤 도시가 아니라, 결국 나의 내부
한가운데였다는 생각이 들 만큼."

한강 "흰"

"질화로에 재가 식어지면
비인 밭에 밤 바람 소리 말을 달리고
엷은 졸음에 겨운
늙으신 아버지가
짚 벼개를 돋아 고이시는 곳
그곳이 차마 꿈엔들 잊힐리야"

정지용 "향수"

"Certain words bleed through to the unwritten pages."

"And these are only the books:
The thing already ambered, capable of waiting, turned to words."

—from *Given Sugar, Given Salt* by Jane Hirshfield

"On one side of the balance is the need for home, for the deep solid roots of place and belonging; on the other is the desire for travel and motion, for the single separate spark of the self freely moving forward, out into time, into the great absorbing stream of the world."

—from *Still life with Oysters and Lemon* by Mark Doty

"Art is an experience, not an object."

—Robert Motherwell

"Indeed, what credit would snow deserve for being white if its matter were not black, if it did not come from the depths of its hidden being to crystallize into its whiteness? Material imagination, which always has a demiurgic tonality, would create white matter from dark matter and seem gratuitous or false to clear thought. But the reverie of material intimacy does not follow the laws of denotative thought."

—from *On Poetic Imagination and Reverie* by Gaston Bachelard

"It is extremely hard to live with silence. The real silence is death, and this is terrible. To approach this silence, it is necessary to journey to the desert. You do not go to the desert to find identity, but to lose it, to lose your personality, to be anonymous. You make yourself void. You become silence. You become more silent than the silence around you. And then something extraordinary happens: you hear silence speak."

—from *The Book of Margins* by Edmond Jabes

"Books are solitudes in which we meet."

—from *The Faraway Nearby* by Rebecca Solnit

Immigrant Flowers, exhibition view

EPILOGUE

나가는 말

Exiting Words

이리저리 to and fro, here and there, back and forth

이러지도 저러지도 either this or that, between a rock and a hard place, sitting on the fence

산발적인, 산재하는, 돌발적, sporadic, intermittent, infrequent, periodic, erratic, patchy, random
Yikes, oops, damn. [Are these words from the *Dokgo Tak* comic series by Lee Sang-moo, which I read as a kid?]

These words describe my inner state of mind, especially during my many, frequent departures. I reflect on those sporadic experiences and the many troubles that result from decision making, mind-changing, conflicts, and dilemmas, which consequently resulted in my diverse body of hands-on work. Being in between. Departures and arrivals. I have arrived nowhere, so perhaps I never left. Ironically, there is nowhere to turn to now, but home lies within me.

I've heard the saying that "if you go fast, walk alone; if you walk far, walk together." I walked alone fast, but I was also alone when I travelled far. However, I can't stop feeling as if I'm just walking around in a circle. I sat down for just a little while, but I'll get up soon to soar in the sky, moving forward like Dongyi's fellow birds. "Dokgo Tak, get up again like a roly-poly toy! Even if you fall." When I was young, I loved characters in comics like the righteous *Tiger Mask* and the even more just *Golden Bat*. "If you're serious about something, don't give up."

My intention for writing was to explain the background of my artwork, my reasons for creating, or just the work itself, but I ended up grumbling. It reminds me of a few elderly ladies I encountered at the bus stop when I was young. Each would share her family history, the story of the child she lost during the war, the resentment felt towards an estranged son. I just nodded or said, "Ah, yes. . . ." The grandmothers went on self-talking

나가는 말

아뿔싸,

이크, 아뿔싸, 제기랄[꼬마 시절, 이상무 만화의 "독고탁" 시리즈에서 접하던 단어들?]

이 단어들은, 특히 자주 집을 나서는 나의 내면의 정신 상태를 묘사한다. 그런 산발적인 경험과 의사결정, 마음의 변화, 갈등과 딜레마에서 오는 많은 고민들을 반영하고, 결과적으로 다양한 형태의 수작업으로 이어진다.

사이에 끼여 있다. 출발 및 도착. 아무 데도 도착하지 않았기 때문에 나는 아무 데도 떠나지 않았을지도 모른다. 반어적으로, 지금은 돌아갈 곳이 없지만, 집은 내 안에 있다.

"빨리 가려면 혼자 걸어라. 멀리 걸으려면 함께 걸으라."고 들었다. 나는 혼자서 빨리, 멀리도 왔다. 하지만 제자리걸음만 하고 있다는 느낌을 지울 수 없다. 잠시 앉아 있었지만 동이의 동료 기러기들처럼 앞으로 나아가 하늘로 날아오를 것이다. "독고탁, 오뚜기처럼 넘어져도 다시 일어나!" 어려서 정의의 타이거 마스크와 황금 박쥐를 무지 좋아했어. "진심이면 포기하지 마."

작업의 뒷배경, 수작을 하는 이유, 혹 작품 설명의 글을 의도했으나, 넋두리로 끝을 보누나. 주절주절 할 말이 많아진 것이, 어릴 적 버스 정거장에서 만났던 할머니 몇 분이 떠오른다. 당신들의 가족사, 전쟁 중 잃어버린 자식 얘기, 집 나간 아들놈 원망. 난 그냥, 고개 끄덕거리거나, "아, 네..." 하고 있으면 한참을 이어가던 '할무니들'. 외할머니 생각이 나서 내 버스는 지나고, 할머니 버스 올 때까지 기다렸다. 수다 할매, 나도 이렇게 할매가 되어가나 보다. 어쩌다 보니 자서전 같네.

두서도 일관성도 논리도 아무것도 없이 무모한 짓을 벌이려고 한다. 글재주, 말재주 꽝이라, 우리 집 안에서는. 부모님, 언니, 남녀 동생 모두 언변, 글솜씨가 꽤 되는데, 나만 유독 달리네... 어릴 적부터 그랬다. 카메라도 못 바라보니 가족 사진 망치던 아이, 늘상 한 박자 늦고, 좀 모지리라서. 그래도, 지구력은 뛰어나. 글을 쓰는 일도 남에게 읽힐 염려가 따르고, 만들어 가는 작업에도 남의 눈을 의식하게 된다. 예술(시각적 또는 문학적) 창작의 주체가 오로지 나인가? 요즘은 관객이나 독자라는 타인이 부담이다. 글은 마음에서 우러나와 자연스레 쓰는 것이다. 글짓기는 글을 지어내는 행위일 것이다. 글은 써야 하는데, 나는 끄적거리기만 한다. 여기저기 끄적거리니 횡설수설이 심하게 끝을 맺는다...

for some time. Remembering my own grandmother, I waited for the elderly ladies to get onto their buses even though my bus had passed. Chattering grannies, one after another. I guess I'm becoming a similar granny. Somehow this book seems to have become an autobiography.

I am about to launch reckless attempts without any coherence or logic. In my family, my parents, older sister, and younger siblings are all good at speaking and writing. I'm the only one who is not good with words. . . . It's been like that since I was little. The kid who ruined her family photos by looking away from the camera, was always a beat late, and a bit slow. Still, my endurance is excellent. Writing is followed by the fear of being read by others, and I become conscious of others' eyes. When it comes to art—visual or literary—am I the only subject? These days I find strangers, audiences, or readers to be a burden. Writing comes naturally from the heart. Writing is an act of creating a text. I write, but I seem to just scribble. Now, as I leave a bunch of gibberish here and there, I make my exit. . . .

Blooming, Withering, and Other Thoughts, detail

Our Country, Good Country, 2023, ceramic

CREDITS

Publisher: Kim Hyung-geun

Translator: Dury Moon

Editor: Che Taejin

Copy editor: Tannith Kriel

Designer: Jung Hyun-young

CATALOG PUBLICATION FUNDED PARTIALLY by

2023 MSU HARP Production Award   MICHIGAN STATE UNIVERSITY

[Michigan State University Humanities & Arts Research Program]

2022-23 RESEARCH/RESIDENCY SUPPORTED/ FUNDED BY

2023 Fulbright Scholarship Award, US Department of State   FULBRIGHT

2023 Archie Bray Foundation, Invited Visiting Artist, Helena, MT

2023 Tinan National University of the Arts, Visiting Artist, Tainan, Taiwan

2023 Atelier L-Imprimerie, GodeLee Collaborative Project, Lausanne, Switzerland

2022 MSU HARP Development Award   MICHIGAN STATE UNIVERSITY

PHOTOGRAPHY CREDITS

Christiane Nill [Germany, Switzerland] p. 36, 73, 77R, 78, 79

Chales Benoit [Michigan, US] p. 9, 83, 85

Hyungduk Shin [Clayarch Gimhae Museum, Korea] p. 97, 101

The Clay Studio [Philadelphia, US] p. 106

Kelly Salchow MacArthur poster design p. 81 [right]

Penn State University poster design p. 81 [left]

IS HERE THERE?

Published in 2024 by Seoul Selection
B1, 6 Samcheong-no, Jongno-gu, Seoul 03062, Korea

Phone: +82-2-734-9567
Fax: 070-8668-1090
Email: hankinseoul@gmail.com
Website: www.seoulselection.com

ISBN: 979-11-89809-67-6 03810

여기가 거긴가?

1판 1쇄 발행 2024년 2월 20일

등록   2003년 1월 28일(제1-3169호)
주소   서울시 종로구 삼청로 6 출판문화회관 지하 1층 (우110-190)
편집부   전화 02-734-9567 팩스 02-734-9562
영업부   전화 02-734-9565 팩스 02-734-9563
홈페이지   www.seoulselection.com

ⓒ 2024 이재원

ISBN: 979-11-89809-67-6 03810